A.L.O.E.

Beyond the Black Waters

A tale

A.L.O.E.

Beyond the Black Waters
A tale

ISBN/EAN: 9783337027070

Printed in Europe, USA, Canada, Australia, Japan

Cover: Foto ©Andreas Hilbeck / pixelio.de

More available books at **www.hansebooks.com**

"' I would tell you everything.' said Oscar, ' were not your peace
dearer to me than my own.'"

"Oscar gave in the letter with a hand that did not tremble.

Page 175

T. NELSON AND SONS
London, Edinburgh, and New York

BEYOND THE BLACK WATERS

A Tale

BY

A. L. O. E.,

Author of " Pictures of St. Peter in an English Home,"
" Driven into Exile," " Harold's Bride,"
" War and Peace,"
&c. &c.

London
THOMAS NELSON AND SONS
35 Paternoster Row
EDINBURGH, AND NEW YORK
1890

Preface.

THE title of this work would probably convey no definite idea to the minds of most Europeans; it might be considered as merely a figurative expression. It is otherwise with the native of Hindostan. The Black Waters are to him those that cut off from happiness and home the criminals of that vast region to which he belongs. Beyond the Black Waters lie the Andaman Islands, where, at the present time, about *thirteen thousand* convicts of both sexes—thieves, murderers, and murderesses—endure the punishment of exile, the due reward of their crimes.

A kind of mysterious pall seems to hang over the isles beyond the Black Waters. The convicts are under Government protection and Government control; nor can there be communication with them (at any rate with those confined in jail) without Government permission. The criminals are not treated harshly; the place of their exile is fruitful and fair. Nature smiles upon the Andaman Islands; it is man, guilty man, who seems to have forgotten how to smile.

To turn to a brighter part of the background of my tale : the stories of the Karens, their traditions, and of the remarkable man who stands amongst them conspicuous as a lighthouse at night, are no invention of mine. These belong to fact and not to fiction. If I would fain awaken pity for the sinners, I would also kindle admiration for the saints, and a keener and more practical interest in England and America for missionary labours in the lands of the East.

Contents.

BEYOND
THE BLACK WATERS.

CHAPTER I.

NEWLY ARRIVED.

"You'll see it, Mr. Lawrence, you'll see it—everything will be changed in England now that the old king is dead and the sailor William on the throne. The people are mad for changes, and shout for reform, as if it meant bread to their butter, or rather beef-steaks and plum-pudding."

"But the Duke——" began Mr. Lawrence; but Dr. Pinfold cut him short ere he could finish the sentence.

"The Iron Duke is facing the mob like a man, but he'll have to give way to popular excitement. Westminster is not Waterloo; let Londoners roar as they will, he can't say, 'Up, Guards, and at them.' The Duke can no more stem the current than he can stop with his field-marshal's baton one of those new-fangled monster engines which crushed out poor Huskisson's life."

The two gentlemen who were discoursing on politics were the chaplain of Moulmein and the doctor of the station. Their path was along a cactus-bordered road, where every here and there the plantain waved its broad green leaves aloft, as if proud of the heavy clusters of fruit forming below. The two men were very different in appearance: the clergyman was small, slight, pale, and fair-haired; the doctor was somewhat portly, with grizzled eyebrows and a copious beard. He was full of the subject of politics, to which Mr. Lawrence gave very divided attention.

"Every ship from England brings stirring tidings," continued the doctor. "Have you seen the papers to-day?"

"Not yet," replied the chaplain. "I was rather absorbed in the perusal of home letters. I am by no means indifferent to what is passing in the dear old island at the other end of the world; but the sounds of political changes, roaring mobs, and exciting orations in London, only reach me here at Moulmein as the distant plash of surges breaking on the shore."

"So it is," observed the doctor philosophically. "What is near always affects us most, a button close to the eye shuts out the landscape, and excludes even the sun. It is of more importance to me that my *bhansamar* should cook my *pillau* to my taste than

that the Tories should secure a majority in the House.
Perhaps your small parish here in Moulmein (if it can
be called a parish at all)—your handful of soldiers, and
a few scattered Europeans, take up more of your attention than the affairs of England, with Scotland and
Ireland to boot."

"Perhaps so," replied the chaplain; "but my interest
in what concerns Siam and Burmah is by no means
confined to what you call my parish in Moulmein. I
have hearty sympathy to give to our American brethren,
labouring nobly and successfully amongst the native
races."

"The natives!" repeated Dr. Pinfold in a tone of
contempt. "Do you think that all the praying and
preaching in the world can wash the niggers white, or
get the blackness out of their blood? The Yankees
could as easily turn pomegranates into potatoes, or make
monkeys into men."

Mark Lawrence held a different opinion, but he saw
that there would be no use at that time in pressing his
views on the cheerful, corpulent doctor, from whom his
own button of personal comfort shut out the view of
anything of a higher nature. Dr. Pinfold's favourite
maxim was *Live, and let live:* the first, and to him more
important, part of the proverb meaning what is called
good-living—not a mere seat, but a well-cushioned chair;
not simple food, but a banquet, washed down with old
wine. It must be owned that the second clause of the

proverb **was** by no means forgotten. Dr. Pinfold was popular as a medical man ; **and** not without reason, for he was not only clever in his profession, but he took a pleasure in curing his patients. Pinfold liked **to** relieve pain, and to see people happy ; and he had **a** feeling of general goodwill towards all his fellow-countrymen which **passed** for benevolence, though his **charity was ever of the** kind which begins at home, and is limited to a conveniently small circle beyond it.

"**I** wish to **know** something **of the** family who arrived yesterday from England *via* Calcutta — the Coldstreams, **to** whom you are going to introduce me," said Mark Lawrence, **changing** the subject of conversation. "**I** think **that we are now** approaching their bungalow ; **a** very pleasant **dwelling, it appears to** be."

"It's a capital house," observed **the doctor** ; "there's not **a** prettier one in Moulmein. It is fitted up too with perfect taste ; **for, you** see, Oscar Coldstream arranged **everything** himself, and built and ornamented the house for the girl to whom he was engaged, whom he has just brought out as his wife. Coldstream came out first, **two** years ago, to get everything ready ; a sensible plan, to my mind, **for** it is folly to bring a pretty **girl** still in her teens to face all sorts of discomforts in a heathenish country like this."

"What sort of man is Mr. Coldstream ? " inquired Mark Lawrence. "I like to know every member of my flock."

"Oscar Coldstream is not much like a sheep," said the doctor gaily; "more like a vigorous, energetic shepherd, who, like the Jewish hero, could catch a lion by the beard or conquer a giant one day, and sing psalms all the next."

The young chaplain's rather melancholy face brightened with pleasure. "I may find in him a helper then," he observed.

"Yes; Coldstream is one of *your* sort," said Pinfold, with a slight emphasis on the pronoun which implied "not one of *my* sort." "But he's a good fellow, a right good fellow, notwithstanding a little Puritanical strictness. Coldstream is a capital shot; he is a first-rate companion on a shooting expedition—can tell you a story to set you in roars of laughter, and is more lively on cold water than most men are when sipping good wine. He does a good business down at the wharf, and has no lack of rupees to jingle. I saw a good deal of Coldstream last year," continued Dr. Pinfold; "for I am an old friend of the Thorns, the family into which he was going to marry. I had played with his lady-love before she was out of baby-clothes. I used to carry her round and round the room perched on my shoulder. I was proud to act *gee-gee* to the dimpled, laughing, dark-eyed child, whose chubby hand grasped my shaggy poll as her rein. Ha! ha! ha! how missie urged me to speed by vigorous movements of her tiny foot encased in its dainty pink kid shoe! That merry child and I were grand playmates; and even when she was promoted to pinafores, and her clustering curls were imprisoned in braids, Io delighted to challenge me to a game. I see her now—dodging me round chairs, defying me to catch her, hiding, and then betraying her hiding-place by an irrepressible laugh. Coldstream thoroughly enjoyed my long stories about his betrothed. My friendship with the Thorns was the one grand link between us; for if ever a man was over head and ears in love, that man was Oscar Coldstream. Certainly Io is worthy of any man's love."

"And now Mr. Coldstream is a happy married man," observed Lawrence, perhaps with something of envy, for his own hopes had been blighted by one of the letters received from England.

"A married man certainly," replied Dr. Pinfold, "but whether happy or not I cannot yet tell, as I have only seen the pair once since they landed. I went down to the wharf to welcome them to their new home in Moulmein. You know that the ship arrived only yesterday evening. I had not much more time than to shake hands, say a little appropriate nonsense to the pretty little bride, and help to look after the luggage. I shall know more about the wedded couple when I have seen them in their own house."

"Mr. Coldstream no doubt looked very happy," said the chaplain. "He has everything to make life bright."

"He looked very much changed," said the doctor,

with a grave expression on his usually cheerful face. "Coldstream hardly seemed to be the same man as he who, in the wildest spirits, not a year ago, embarked in the ship bound for old England. Such a buoyant step was his, such a sparkling eye, as if the cup of joy awaiting him intoxicated him by anticipation! Certainly there is a difference now."

"What kind of difference?" asked Mark Lawrence.

"The difference between a handsome lamp lighted, and the flame turned up high, and the same lamp turned down, almost extinguished. Oscar looked like his own elder brother—a grave, thoughtful man; not in the least like a jolly bridegroom."

"Perhaps he was ill," suggested the chaplain.

"He said not, for I asked him the question. Then the bonnie bride told me that Coldstream had been very ill just before his marriage, but that he had long ago recovered his health. I've my doubts about that—my doubts about that," continued the doctor, slightly shaking his head in a professional way. "People don't lose flesh and colour at Coldstream's age if there's nothing the matter. I should like to have asked some questions; found out the state of his— But here we are at the house, and yonder's a *koi-hai* to take in your card. I shall not waste my bit of pasteboard; none is needed when you call on a young lady who knows your name as well as her own. I shall be Io's '*Doctor Pinny*' to the end of the chapter."

CHAPTER II.

THE PRODIGY.

THE two visitors were conducted through a long veranda, paved with a delicate mosaic of many-coloured tiles, and overhung with blossoming creepers.

"Coldstream planted every one of these with his own hand," observed the doctor, as his companion stopped for a moment to admire a specially magnificent creeper. "His lady-love always delighted in flowers. She used, when a child, to stick one into each of my button-holes; and would have hung daisy-chains round my neck, but that I was impatient of fetters, even when forged by pretty, plump, dimpled hands." Dr. Pinfold's face always wore a benevolent expression when he thought of the little godchild who had been dear to the old bachelor, and whose innocent affection had been his best tie to his fellow-creatures.

The visitors then entered a pleasant apartment, which looked shady and cool after the glare outside. The white walls were ornamented with the graceful arabesque designs in painting in which Oriental artists excel. There were on them also a few choice water-colour drawings, executed by Mr. Coldstream himself. He had considerable artistic talent, and had been stimulated to make finished pictures from rough sketches taken in England, that his bride might have pleasant reminders of home. The skins of a tiger, a bear, and two leopards, brought down by Oscar's gun, were spread as rugs on the matted floor.

Dr. Pinfold looked around for his friends, but the sole occupant of the apartment was a lad about sixteen or seventeen years of age, who, with a large book open before him, sat with his chin resting on the palms of his thick hands. The youth seemed to be so much absorbed in what he was studying, that he at first hardly noticed the entrance of visitors. Dr. Pinfold on seeing him uttered an exclamation of astonishment rather than of pleasure.

" Why, Thud, *you* here ! is it possible ? " cried the doctor, moving forward and holding out his hand.

The lad who was thus addressed rose slowly, lazily, advanced two steps, and then rather touched than shook the extended hand, almost with the air of one who grudges the trouble of exchanging common civilities.

" What on earth brought you here ?" exclaimed Pinfold.

" Of course one must travel if one wishes to absorb new ideas ; science demands—"

" Oh, never mind science just now," cried the doctor. " Did you come with your brother and sister ? "

"I came with my sister and her husband," was the reply. Thud was glancing at his open book as he spoke, as if he thought time lost in such commonplace conversation.

"How was it that I did not see you yesterday, Thud, when I went to the ship? I did not notice you when I was overhauling the luggage."

"I was not going to overhaul luggage," said Thud, with a touch of contempt in his tone. "I got out of the noise and racket as soon as I could, and took a stroll on the beach to look for conchological specimens."

"Just like you—just like you," muttered the doctor; "always out of the way when anything useful is to be done."

"I'm sometimes in the way," said Thud.

"You never said a truer word in your life, my boy!" cried the doctor laughing. "You are very frequently *in the way* of others."

Thud did not look angry; he was too perfectly satisfied with himself to be sensitive to satire. To hit the lad was like thumping a bag of wool. In looking at Thud the chaplain was irresistibly reminded of an owl. A somewhat beaked nose in the midst of a full round face, half-closed eyes under rounded brows, a low forehead surmounted by a mop of hay-coloured hair, with a trick peculiar to Thud of poising his head a little on one side when any idea of peculiar magnitude weighed on his brain, made him resemble the bird of

Minerva. The large head was planted, almost without the intervention of neck, on a short, thick figure, the legs being particularly curtailed in length. Thud was not, however, a dwarf; and he had a good opinion of his own appearance, as well as of everything else appertaining to himself.

"Where are Mr. Coldstream and Io?" asked the doctor.

"Don't know," was the curt reply; then the young sage condescended to add, "I s'pose they've gone out."

"You'll please to find them," said the doctor a little tartly. "Tell Coldstream that our chaplain, the Rev. Mark Lawrence, has called to see him; and let Io know that her old friend is waiting.—Pray, Mr. Lawrence, take a seat."

"I'll send a servant—" began Thud.

"No, sir, you'll please to go yourself," said the doctor; "you are more likely to find the pair, and more able to explain who have come to see them, than any native could be. Besides, you could not give a message in any tongue but your own; though I daresay that Io has learned a good deal of the language during the voyage from England."

Thud again gave a regretful glance at his book, then slowly and unwillingly quitted the room. The only notice which he took of the chaplain as he passed him was shown by an awkward nod of the head.

"That most unmitigated owl!" exclaimed the doctor,

throwing himself into the most luxurious lounging-chair in the room. " What could have induced Oscar Coldstream to hamper himself with such an incubus as that ? It has been one of his magnanimous acts of self-denial. Coldstream has wished to relieve his bride's widowed mother of the burden of supporting, the worry of trying to manage a conceited, lazy fellow, who is ready enough to eat, and then spout scientific nonsense, but who has never earned a penny in his life, and is never likely to earn one. I see now why poor Coldstream looks so grave and gloomy. I guess that Sindbad the sailor did not feel very lively with the old man of the sea on his back, and Thud would be an even more intolerable burden to any sensible man. Coldstream had, I'll be bound, flared up at some piece of arrogant folly, and—for he has pepper and mustard in him—given his precious brother-in-law a good set down, or maybe a well-earned box on the ear ; then Oscar had seen Io look vexed, and had reproached himself for being hard on the owl, and had ended by begging his pardon ! Coldstream is absurdly conscientious. I can tell you a curious anecdote which shows the nature of the man. Some time last year one of his assistants made a very provoking blunder in a shipping account. Coldstream thought it something worse than a blunder, and taxed the fellow, in the presence of some half a dozen of us, with cooking the accounts. It appeared afterwards, on examination, that the man had been only a fool, not a knave. Would you believe it? Coldstream collected together every individual who had heard his hasty accusation, and in the presence of all made a public apology to his own assistant! I call such conduct a little absurd."

"Honourable—generous!" was the comment of the young chaplain. "I feel impatient to be introduced to your friend."

"You'll find Coldstream a decided improvement on Thud," observed Dr. Pinfold smiling.

"How came the lad by such an uncommon name?" asked Lawrence.

"His real name is Thucydides Thorn," replied Pinfold. "His father, my old school-fellow, was a somewhat eccentric fellow, like his boy. However, he resembled Thud only in this, that he wanted to do everything in a different way from every one else. Beaten paths were Tom Thorn's aversion; he would rather flounder through a bog than walk along a highway. There is a little smack of vanity in this, I take it, Mr. Lawrence; but Tom Thorn was really a clever man. Happily he married a sensible sort of woman, who minded his house, and was not put out if her husband sat up all night star-gazing, or forgot his dinner when studying a Greek poem. Your genius should never marry a genius; one partner in the matrimonial firm should serve as ballast, if the other be all inflated sail."

Pinfold paused, and the chaplain's faint smile expressed assent. Then the doctor went on with his story.

"The first child born was a girl. Tom Thorn did not think much of the little creature who came when he was translating Euripides and disturbed him by her squalling: she was called Jane, after her mother. The father was a bit disappointed that the little brat was not a boy. Then came a second girl—another disappointment; but she turned out to be a little beauty, so Thorn consoled himself by giving her the classic name of Io. I thought the name absurd, till some twenty months afterwards I heard it from the cherry lips of the little prattler who bore it. Io always made two distinct syllables of the two letters, leaning on the first; and I found that the word was charming. One day—she was just four years old, and wearing her pink birthday sash—Io came running to me with the grand news that some one, she thought perhaps an angel, had brought her a baby brother. The little pet's eyes sparkled with joy; she danced about the room with delight: she could not know that poor Thud was hardly the gift that an angel would be likely to bring. This boy, whom Thorn expected to turn out a genius, was christened Thucydides, this being a name which 'nobody can speak, and nobody can spell.' It was soon shortened to Thud. So Thud, theoretical Thud, the boy will be to the end of his days."

"I suppose, from what I have seen and heard of the lad, that it was rather the father than the mother who conducted his education," observed Mr. Lawrence.

" Education ! " repeated the doctor, with a very signifi-
cant compression of his full lips and a turning down of
the corners of his mouth. " Thud was fed on poly-
syllables instead of pap, caught the trick of his father's
dogmatic manner, and lisped nonsense with the air of a
Solon. Of course the boy was too clever to be much
troubled with a Primer ; I think his found its way into
the fire. When Thud could neither read nor write he
was watching his father's scientific experiments ; for with
Thorn, who was an erratic genius, classics had given
way to science, and his whole mind was full of theories
about electric currents. I remember his boy at dinner
one day (we were never free from his presence and
prating at meals), when the pudding had been somewhat burnt in the oven. Master Thud (he still wore a
bib) pushed away his plate, and gave out his authoritative
dictum, ' Pudding ought to be cooked by electricity.'
Thorn looked with parental pride on his hopeful prodigy.
' Depend upon it, Pinfold,' he said to me across the table,
' that boy will make his mark.' I could not help making the sarcastic observation, ' Folk who make their
mark are those who don't know how to write.' Then
turning towards the little prig—' What do you know
about electricity ? ' I asked. ' I knows *all* about the
electric—' The boy stopped ; the ' currents ' would not
come to the juvenile memory. But Thud never lost his
self-assurance. ' I knows all about the electric *gooseberries,*' came out, as if all the wisdom of a Newton

were crammed into that heavy head. We all burst out laughing, **Thud** laughing the loudest of all. I believe that he thought that he had said a remarkably clever thing. **Ha! ha! ha!**"

"**I** daresay that electric gooseberries became proverbial in the family," observed the chaplain smiling.

"**This is but a** specimen anecdote," continued the doctor. "Master **Thucydides Thud was** always

> ' As who should say, I am Sir Oracle,
> And when I speak—let no dog bark.'

And Coldstream **has actually** brought out this owl to hoot in Moulmein!"

CHAPTER III.

DEAD OR ALIVE?

THE conversation was interrupted by the return of Thud, who seemed to be slightly excited, though his visage usually expressed nothing but self-satisfaction, the solemn look befitting one with an inward consciousness that he was seated in a professor's chair to enlighten the world with his wisdom.

"What's the matter, boy?" asked the doctor quickly. "Where are Io and her husband?"

"Looking after a wretched native woman whom an ox has gored and trampled upon," replied Thud. "If Oscar had not rushed up and broken his umbrella over the brute, the woman would have been killed outright. I think that she *is* killed," continued the lad, "or more than half. You never saw such a horrid rush of blood from the wound! Io tied her silk scarf round the woman to stop it;—the scarf will have to be thrown away. 'Tis no use to try to save the creature. I've a theory,"—Thud had relapsed into his natural, or rather unnatural manner,—"that when people are at the last gasp it's better to leave them to die in peace."

"We'll remember your counsel when an ox gores you," said the doctor tartly. He had risen from his seat on hearing of the accident, taken up his solar topi and umbrella, and was about to start with the chaplain to see if his surgical skill could avail.

"No use in going out; they are all coming into the veranda," said Thud. "I informed them that the doctor was here."

Dr. Pinfold gave rapid orders to a native servant who was waiting outside regarding things which might be needed in a surgical case. Whilst he was speaking, Oscar, with another man, bore into the veranda the slight form of a Karen woman. Her long black hair hung over Mr. Coldstream's supporting shoulder, her garments were dabbled with blood, her eyes were closed; the poor creature gave no sign of life, not even a groan. A little Karen girl, some ten or twelve years of age, weeping as if her heart would break, hung over the *charpai* on which her mother was now laid—the simple light bedstead which is so easily carried, and which in the East seems to be always at hand. It had been brought from a servant's house in the compound by the order of Oscar.

"Bring water—brandy!" cried Dr. Pinfold. Io was off in a moment and quickly brought both, whilst the doctor was examining the fearful wound of the patient.

The glass was put to the poor woman's lips, but they did not unclose; the liquid ran down on either side of the mouth, not a drop was taken in. The eyes under those heavy lids would never see the daylight again.

"No use; all's over—she's gone!" said Dr. Pinfold, after pressing his fingers on her wrist to feel the pulse which no longer beat. He saw that the woman was dead. "Nothing remains to be done but to carry off the body for burial."

"So soon!" exclaimed Io in a tone of expostulation. "Is it not possible that life may linger?"

"Life is quite extinct," said the doctor.

"She is deceased—annihilated—I told you so," joined in Thud.

"We bury quickly in these latitudes," observed Dr. Pinfold; "and it would not be well to keep a corpse in the house to which Coldstream has just brought his bride."

"See, the veranda is desecrated by blood-stains," said Thud, "and so is Io's apparel."

"Go and change it, my love," cried Oscar with a look of pain almost amounting to horror.

"A few minutes—just let me stay a few minutes to try to comfort this poor child," said Io. "Let me try to find out from her whether she has a father, brother, any protector, or whether she is alone in this wide, wide world." Putting her arm round the sobbing girl, Io spoke to her in tender tones and in her own language,

to the great surprise of Dr. Pinfold. Io's words were
evidently understood; for while preparations were being
made for the removal of the corpse, Io drew from the
young Karen the fact that she **had no** father, no relation—that to her that dead mother had indeed been all
in all. The girl clung to the body with wild tenacity,
heedless **of all that** the chaplain, doctor, or Oscar could
say; yet, with a kind of instinctive obedience, loosened
her hold when Io laid her white **hand on the** brown one.
Then the child fell weeping at the feet of the lady, and
kissed the hem of her blood-stained robe.

"O Oscar dearest, if we can find no relation, will you
not let me adopt this poor child?" said Mrs. Coldstream,
her bright eyes dewy with tears.

"Do whatever your kind heart prompts you to do,"
was her husband's reply. "Your will is law here. The
girl shall be brought up as your little attendant."

Io persuaded the young Karen to follow her to her
own apartment, and Oscar and Mr. Lawrence made
arrangements for the removal of the body on the
charpai. The two Englishmen needed no introduction
to each other, meeting, as they did, under such solemn
circumstances beside the form of the dead. Mark
Lawrence had been prepared to like Mr. Coldstream;
and now Oscar's brave though fruitless attempt to save
a poor native, and the fact that he had himself carried
her lifeless body, roused a feeling of admiration in the
heart of the lonely pastor which seemed certain to

warm into friendship. Mark thought that he had at
last found one to share his interests and cares, some one
whose sympathy would lighten his burdens. He looked
at the high pale brow and the fine features of Coldstream, and felt that he had never met with so interesting a man. Oscar's gentle courtesy to his wife had not
escaped the chaplain's notice; and Mark silently thanked
God for having sent to Moulmein a pair whose friendship might, even to a disappointed man like himself,
make life a less sad and weary thing.

The two gentlemen went out to walk together, and
Thud chose to make an unwelcome third. Oscar and
Mark found their conversation perpetually interrupted
by pedantic remark or tiresome question. Thud wanted
to give Mr. Lawrence an early impression of his own
remarkable sagacity and knowledge, and only succeeded
in producing a conviction that Coldstream must be a
model of self-denial to make his roof-tree a perch for
such a self-conceited owl.

CHAPTER IV.

THE MYSTERIOUS CLOUD.

" I'LL wait and see Io and have a talk with her," said
Dr. Pinfold, as he again made himself comfortable in
the easy-chair, after possessing himself of a newspaper
which happened to lie on the table.   It was full of
political articles and news, but just then politics had
little attraction for Dr. Pinfold.   He was thinking a
great deal of his god-daughter Io—recalling the old
times when she used to sit on his knee, and dive in his
pocket for the sweets which he took care that she
should find there.   Pinfold wanted a long talk, a con-
fidential talk with his favourite, and was as much
relieved by the absence of Thud as the other gentlemen
were troubled by his presence.

Io did not know that her old friend was waiting, and
it was some time before she made her appearance in
fluttering garments white as snow, over which fell her
auburn ringlets.   The fair lady smiled with pleasure at
finding her old doctor still in the room, and took a low
seat close beside him.

"She looks lovelier than ever," thought Dr. Pinfold.

"It was very good in you to wait so long," said Mrs. Coldstream. "I have kept you an unreasonable time, but I could not quiet the poor child at once. Now she has cried herself to sleep."

"How is it that you could talk to her, my rosebud?" asked the doctor. "I was astonished to hear you speak Karen. I know hardly anything of that language myself, just enough to ask a few medical questions when Karens find their way to the dispensary. These people are scattered amongst the Siamese and Burmese like poppies amongst corn."

"Which are the poppies, which the corn?" asked Io in her old playful way. "From what Oscar has told me, it seems that these Karens are a race whom both Siamese and Burmese conspire to oppress, but who are more to be trusted than either."

"It may be so," said the doctor.

"My smattering of their language is easily accounted for," continued Io. "On my husband's first return to England, nearly three years ago, he brought with him a little Karen boy, whom he had rescued from some horrid Siamese tyrant. After our engagement, when Oscar was obliged to return to Moulmein, he left this boy in my charge, the poor little fellow being too ill to travel."

"A kind of big keepsake to keep your lover in mind, I suppose," observed Pinfold, "like a miniature framed in ebony."

"I liked the child for his own sake as well as his master's," said Io. "I talked a great deal with him, taught him something, and he taught me his language in return. I was sorry that he only knew Karen, for that is not what is most spoken here; but I thought that to learn it was better than learning nothing, and, curiously enough, the first native in Moulmein with whom I have to do is a Karen. You cannot think how much pleased I was when I found myself understood by the motherless girl."

"You'll be making a match one of these days between your two brown *protégés*," said the doctor gaily.

"Ah no; the poor dear boy sleeps in an English churchyard," replied Io with a sigh. "Oscar has had a little monument placed over his grave—a cross, for the boy died a Christian."

"Well, now, let us speak of Oscar himself," said the doctor, who felt little interest in the death and burial of a brown Karen boy. "I want you to answer some questions about his health, for he has grown paler, and thinner, and graver. It is not natural that a man should look ten years older in less than ten months. Do you think that your husband is ill?"

The doctor almost wished the question unspoken, for it brought such a look of distress to his favourite's face. Io, however, answered clearly and distinctly every interrogation; she had been longing to consult her experienced old friend.

"Eats as usual, you say; complains of no pain; can take a great deal of exercise; seems to have lost no physical strength! How do you account for his altered looks?"

"I suppose that I must tell you everything, dear god-father," said Io, resting her clasped hands on the arm of the doctor's chair; "indeed it is a great comfort to be able to consult you. How often I have wished to do so when you were far away! You know how happy, how very happy we were at the time of our engagement, for you were in England then, before Oscar returned to Moulmein."

"You both seemed perfectly satisfied with the number which you had drawn in life's lottery," said the doctor smiling; "till the gilding wears off the prize, I suppose that lovers usually are so. Coldstream was certainly proud of what he had won, and bore with a fair amount of philosophy all the jests and banter of your madcap cousin Walter Manly."

"Ah, poor Walter!" sighed Io; then she continued her narration :—"Of course our first parting was a great trial, but I need not dwell upon that; we looked forward to meeting again, and the arrival of Oscar's letters was a frequent source of delight. At last the time of separation drew to a close. Oscar wrote, 'I shall, please God, arrive almost as soon as this letter. Be sure that you send me a welcome by the pilot.' We knew that Oscar would land at Dover, for our house was scarce two miles from the castle. I need not say how I counted the days, how I watched every large vessel coming up the Channel. As we could not tell the exact time when the *Argus* would arrive, I prepared a long letter to be sent to the office at Portsmouth to greet Oscar before he should quit the vessel, as it was arranged that the pilot should take it. A very long journal letter it was—"

"Containing sweet things, as the white comb holds honey?" asked the playful doctor.

Io slightly blushed as she replied, "There were all sorts of things in my letter: scraps of news—whatever amused me, and I thought would amuse Oscar. I remember that I wrote of various friends, and of presents which I had received. I told of the favourite hunter on which Walter won the steeplechase—"

"Ah, that Walter!" interrupted the doctor; "I prophesied years ago that he would break his neck in some wild prank!"

."Your prophecy came but too true," said Io sadly. "You must have heard of the foolish bet which cost him his life."

"Ay, ay; he would climb up some inaccessible cliff," observed Pinfold. "I read about it in the papers at the time. But let us return to the subject of Oscar."

"We had arranged that a swift messenger should bring us instant news when the *Argus* came in sight," continued Io; "but a sea-fog prevented the vessel's being seen until she was almost in port;—she was to touch at Dover on her way up Channel. Not many minutes elapsed between my hearing of Oscar's arrival and my seeing him myself."

" You had a joyful meeting of course," said the doctor.

Io's head drooped, and she pressed her hand over her dark eyes, as if to hide some painful object. She was for some moments unable to speak.

" You must tell me all," said the doctor. " How can a medical man possibly judge of a case unless he knows all the symptoms ? "

Io, with her eyes still covered, made reply in a hurried, tremulous tone,—

" I shall never forget that evening. It was about an hour after sunset, and dark, but the servant was bringing in the lamps. A wild February wind had succeeded the fog—such a boisterous wind ; it disturbed me, for I was straining my ear to catch the sound of a messenger's feet, and the howling and shrieking of the blast which had suddenly risen drowned all other noises. It seemed an instinct which made me run to the hall door and open it. I was almost thrown down by the gust which rushed in and extinguished the lamp which I held in my hand. But there was the messenger indeed, and I thought of—cared for—nothing else. I cried, ' Is the *Argus* in ? ' I could scarcely make the question heard, but the answer made me the happiest woman on earth.

I flew to my mother and sister, and proposed that we should all go forth and meet the newly arrived, for he would not tarry on the way. My mother and Jane expostulated, and spoke of the storm, which was increasing ; but I rather enjoyed the rough weather, for the wind had speeded the *Argus.*"

Pinfold suspected, and with reason, that Io lingered over these unnecessary details in order to postpone some painful disclosure. As she paused with a gasp, he observed, " I suppose that your lover appeared before you had persuaded your good mother to go forth in the darkness and storm."

" He appeared," said Io, and paused again.

" How did he appear ? I really must know," said the doctor.

" It was dreadful—too dreadful to tell," faltered Io. " The hall was dark, except for light which came from a room that was sheltered from the wild wind. A form came—almost staggered in ; I could scarcely see the face, but I knew that it was Oscar's. ' Oh, I am so glad that you have come ! ' I exclaimed, running to meet him. ' *Are you glad ?* ' he cried, in a voice quite unlike his own. Oscar caught hold of both my wrists, as if to push me from him, stumbled, and fell down at my feet, almost dragging me down in his fall."

" Extraordinary, most extraordinary ! " exclaimed the doctor ; " do you think that he was in a fit ? "

" Something like it, I suppose, for Oscar had to be

raised, like a dead weight, and carried into the drawing-room, which we had just left, and laid on the sofa. **Of** course we sent at once for the nearest medical man, who bled him at once."

" That looked like **a fit**," observed **Pinfold.** " Did the bleeding soon bring him to himself ?"

" Yes ; Oscar awoke, **but it** was a terrible awaking. I do not like to speak, even to think of **that** fearful night and the painful days which followed." Io's voice was choked by **a** sob, **and** tear-drops forced their way between the slender fingers which concealed the **upper** part of her face.

" I want to know the symptoms **of the** disease ;— I suppose that you helped to nurse **him.** **Was** Cold-stream like one suffering from brain-fever ?" **asked the** doctor.

" He would not let me nurse him," murmured **Io, in** an almost inaudible voice ; " he could not endure to have me near him—that was the worst trial of all."

Dr. Pinfold looked exceedingly grave ; his experience told him that this symptom was of a very alarming nature. As a medical man, he knew that hatred shown towards the very being once most tenderly loved is a not unfrequent sign of madness.

" **My poor** child!" said Dr. Pinfold, as he laid his hand gently on the soft auburn ringlets of the young head drooping beside him ; " how long did this painful phase **of** the malady last ?"

" It seemed to me for ages," said Io, " but I believe for
not many days. I used to wander in misery up and
down the passage into which opened the door which I
dared not enter. My mother, herself suffering from a
recent bereavement, nursed my Oscar. Everything that
could possibly excite or distress him was kept from him.
He was not told of the death in our family; nor of the
breaking of the bank in which all our small property
had been lodged, so that, except my mother's trifling
pension, absolutely nothing remained. Oscar knew not
of our trouble, our poverty. He never asked questions;
he scarcely ever uttered a word."

" Madness," said the doctor to himself; then he asked
the question aloud, " What broke this spell of silence ? "

" I went one day into our little parlour to get pen
and ink to write a note to the medical man. I saw
papers of Thud's lying about,—he often writes on scraps
or backs of letters. My eyes fell on a sealed letter
which I recognized at once. Its outside was scribbled
all over with some calculation made by Thud, but I
knew my own handwriting in the address. The letter
was directed to O. Coldstream, Esq., passenger on board
the *Argus;* to be forwarded by the pilot-boat. The
letter had never been opened—never sent; Thud had
forgotten to take it to the post."

" He deserved to have his neck wrung ! " cried the indignant doctor. " What did you do on discovering your
letter ? "

Io uncovered her eyes; she looked pale, but her manner was calmer than before. "The sight of that letter gave me a gleam of hope," she said. "I could now see some kind of reason for Oscar's displeasure. I had promised to write by the pilot, and I had apparently broken my word."

"An absurd reason for a man's behaving like a maniac," said Dr. Pinfold; "but those in love sometimes act like fools. What did you do when you found the letter?"

"I said to myself, 'This is my last chance of re-gaining his—what I have lost. I *will* venture into the room: I *will* have a full explanation.'"

"Go on, go on," said Pinfold, with impatient interest.

"Oscar was seated writing at a table, for he was not then confined to a sick-bed; indeed he hardly ever went to sleep, but, night and day, paced up and down his apartment. Summoning all the courage I could, I walked straight up to Oscar,—I felt my life's happiness was at stake,—and I silently laid my letter on the table before him. Oscar started at the sight of the address, and eagerly, almost passionately, tore the letter open. His hand trembled violently as he read the contents. I could not see his face, for I stood behind him; but Oscar knew that I was there. Suddenly he started up from his seat and faced me. 'You did then love me!' he exclaimed. 'More than life,' I answered. 'Oh that I had received this before!' cried Oscar, with a sound like a convulsive sob; and he took me into his arms—to his heart."

"Now, this is a very romantic story, very," said Dr. Pinfold, speaking partly to give Io time to recover from her agitation; "but to an old bachelor like myself it seems incomprehensible that a man, a sensible man too, should make himself and every one else wretched merely because a letter miscarried. Dry your eyes, dear, and tell me the rest. I suppose that after the explanation all went merry as a marriage bell."

"More like a funeral bell," sighed Io. "Oscar became well—that is, he recovered his bodily health, but not his spirits. He joined us in the sitting-room, he was willing to have me constantly near him, but he never asked me to settle a time for our marriage. Oscar never even entered on the subject; which distressed my poor mother, who was beginning to be in actual straits. Then my mother and Jane consulted together, and agreed that Oscar must be told of the breaking of the bank and the loss of our fortunes. It was only honourable to let him know that if he wedded me at all, it would be as a portionless bride. Of course I was anxious that Oscar should be made aware of our losses."

"How did he take the news?" asked the doctor.

"Hearing of our poverty seemed to be to him almost a consolation. With more animation than he had shown in his manner since his illness, my dear generous Oscar told me how much gratified he would be if my mother would permit him to settle on her an annual allowance, and, to give him some right to such a privilege, he asked if I would name a day when he might call me his wife."

"Just like him—just like him," said Pinfold; "and Coldstream cumbered himself with your precious brother into the bargain."

"That was such a relief to my mother," said Io. "Oscar promised to help to educate Thud himself, and to try to procure for him some little employment here."

"And that after the fellow had played you such an owlish trick with the letter!" exclaimed Pinfold. "I should have been tempted to kick him downstairs. And how did Master Thud get on with his studies under your husband?" The doctor wanted to coax a smile into his god-daughter's face.

"Not very well, I must confess. The studies were begun on board ship, and Oscar was wonderfully patient; but when he attempted to teach, Thud was determined to argue. I believe that he considers himself to be a good deal more clever than Oscar. Thud says that philosophers are born, not made."

"The only way to make that boy do anything for his own living is to treat him as they do young dogs,—fling him into the middle of a pond to teach him to swim."

"But what if the poor dog should sink?" observed Io.

"Likely enough, with a mill-stone of nonsensical theories hanging about his neck," cried the doctor; "but there is no other plan that has a chance of success.

Turn Thud out of your comfortable house, for he will never work as long as he can eat good mutton at your table, without even the trouble of carving the slice. But now, let's return to the subject of your wedding," continued Pinfold, for, looking at Coldstream's conduct from a medical point of view, he was anxious for precise information.

"Ours was a very, very quiet wedding," said Io gravely.

"But Coldstream did not do anything—very peculiar?" inquired the medical man.

"No," said Io, with a little hesitation; "only, when he took my hand in church,—it was on a hot day in June,—his felt cold as ice, cold as the hand of a corpse."

"Strange, very strange!" muttered Pinfold under his breath, as he tried to recall to mind any similar case. "Do you see any change in him as regards other matters?" he asked, looking keenly at the young wife.

"No—except—I'd rather not say," replied Io, a flush rising to her pale cheek.

"But it is as a medical adviser that I wish to know all," said Pinfold.

"This has nothing to do with medical matters. I do not wish to say more; I have had as much as I can bear," said Io, rising from her low seat.

The doctor felt that it was time to end the interview, which had caused a most painful strain on his young friend. He also rose, and bade Io good-bye in his own lively manner, which, however, was a little forced on the present occasion. The good-natured doctor looked grave enough as he passed through the flower-mantled veranda.

" Poor fellow ! poor fellow !" he muttered to himself. " I never heard that there was insanity in the Coldstream family. I must try to find out; but it would be awkward to ask a man like Mr. Coldstream whether either of his parents was ever in a lunatic asylum. Perhaps Oscar had a touch of the sun during his voyage in the *Argus.* I should like to question on this point one of his fellow-passengers. As good luck will have it, yonder comes Pogson, who went home in that vessel on short leave to see a sick mother. I'll hail him, and ask a question or two, to decide the point of sunstroke. If Coldstream had a sharp one, that might account for all."

The young man called Pogson, a clerk in Government employ, approached, taking a cigar from his mouth to return the greeting of the doctor.

" Pogson, you went home in the *Argus* with Coldstream ? " said Pinfold, almost as soon as the two met.

" Yes, we went home together ; but I had to return earlier than he did," was Pogson's reply.

" Had Coldstream any illness, anything like sunstroke on the voyage ? " asked the doctor.

" Not he ; no one had better health," replied Pogson.

" But he was a bit melancholy, perhaps—had occasional fits of depression ? "

Pogson burst out laughing at the question. " Coldstream was merry as a lark," he said. "He was the life and soul of our party."

"Then there must be a taint of hereditary madness," mused Pinfold, as he again went on his way. "I don't pretend to be a saint, like Coldstream, but I do say this for myself, that had I been in his place I would not have done so unprincipled, so cruel a thing as to have linked my fortunes with those of a bright, happy, trusting young creature like Io!"

CHAPTER V.

ANCIENT TRADITIONS.

Io had been obliged in her interview with a medical
adviser to give a detailed account of occurrences which
had caused her the keenest pain; she had had to draw
back a curtain to reveal a picture of the past on which
it was agony to gaze. But Io's naturally bright and
buoyant disposition did not allow her to nurse her griefs
for the past and her fears for the future, as some
sufferers seem to find a morbid satisfaction in doing.
The curtain was dropped again over the picture of woe.
" Let the past be—as far as possible—forgotten; and
for the future," thus mused Io, " is there not a pitying
Father who hath promised that all things shall work
together for good to them that love Him? Can I not
trust that promise, and so lay down my burden of fears?
I have so much, so very much, to make me thankful and
happy. I am the cherished wife of one of the noblest
of men. Oscar has wonderfully recovered from his distressing illness, and though everything is not yet bright,
I believe—yes, I do believe—that joy is coming. I

will trust, and not be afraid; but oh! I would give all that I have in the world to hear Oscar laugh again."

Io was like the fair lily which refuses to sink though the waters encompass it around. It lifts its bright head above them all, and smiles in the face of the sun. It even covers over those dark waters with the verdant leaves of hope; and if some drops, like tears, rest on the spreading leaves, even those tears, like diamonds, glitter in the light. It seemed less impossible to Io than it is to most people to *rejoice always*, for her trustful, restful spirit had found the secret of peace.

Mrs. Coldstream had also a perpetual source of pleasure in giving pleasure, of comfort in comforting others. She found delight in receiving the poor Karen as a gift from God. Mah-A (Io shortened the name to Maha) was something to cherish, to make happy, to lead to God, even as the Karen boy had been. Io was not self-absorbed; she knew little of that concentration of the mind on one's own desires, pleasures, even failings, which perpetually drives the mind back on the centre of self. The natural flow of Io's thoughts was outward and upward—towards the many whom she loved upon earth, and the One whom she worshipped in heaven. Thus Io rarely lacked something to make her happy, and she was constantly adding to the happiness of others.

Poor bereaved Maha could not resist the fascination of that loving manner, that winsome smile, which was to her sore heart like balm on a bleeding wound. The young Karen intuitively clung to her young mistress, and delighted to sit at her feet. As Maha looked up trustfully into Io's face, Mrs. Coldstream thought that the dark eyes raised towards her were lovely; that there was beauty in the clearly-pencilled eyebrows and the fine, albeit tangled, black hair. Perhaps others would not have thought Maha pretty—Thud called her a flat-nosed fright—but none could deny that the young Karen's figure was perfectly formed, and that her movements were graceful. The girl's voice, too, was soft and melodious.

"I am going to try to teach Maha a little about our blessed religion," said Io to her husband one morning at breakfast.

"I've a theory that natives cannot understand anything that they cannot manipulate with their hands and masticate with their teeth," was the formal dictum of Thud. "They cannot even imagine a god unless they see some hideous image with black face and half-a-dozen arms."

"Karens are said to be free from idolatry," was Coldstream's quiet observation.

"Oh, people may say so, but I don't believe it," said Thucydides Thorn. "I'm trying to discover why all brown and black skinned nations worship idols." Thud's head was poised a little on one side, for this was a weighty subject.

"You had better make sure that your theory, what-

ever it may be, is founded on facts," observed Coldstream.

"Theories first, facts come afterwards," said Thud
solemnly—an observation which made Oscar faintly
smile, and Io burst into a silvery laugh.

"You will next have a theory that trees should be planted
root upwards, and people walk on their heads!" cried she.

"You need not laugh," said Thud, a little offended;
"you women know nothing of logic. I can prove my
assertion to be correct. Pray, which comes first—a
thought, or an act?"

"The thought, if it prompt the act," replied Io.

"There, I have caught you!" cried Thud triumphantly.
"Theories are thoughts, and acts are facts; so facts must
be founded on theories, not theories on facts;" and
confident that he had gained a victory, and said something very logical and clever, Thucydides quitted the
room, carrying his heavy head as high as his very short
neck would allow.

After attending to household arrangements, Io called
her dear little Karen to take her first Scripture lesson.
"I had better commence from the beginning," thought
the lady, as she placed her large picture book on the
sofa open at the representation of the serpent tempting
Eve. Maha took her seat on the ground at her lady's
feet, and surveyed the picture—the first which she ever
had seen—with grave and thoughtful eyes.

"I am going to tell you a little of what is written in

God's great book, the Bible," began Io in broken Karen, which was, however, almost always intelligible to the young girl. "I am going to tell you how sin and sorrow came into the world. You see the woman in the picture: she was the first who ever lived on earth, and she is our mother—yours and mine. She lived with her husband in a beautiful garden. God placed them there—the great God who made and who loves us all."

"I know that story," said Maha quietly. "All we Karens who come from Bassein know it; our fathers told it to us, as their fathers told it to them."

"What did they tell?" asked Io with interest, wondering whether it were possible that any legend of the Fall could exist amongst a race who, but a short time before, had not even a written language.

"Does the sahiba wish to hear the whole story of the first man and woman who lived in the garden?" asked Maha.

"Tell me everything that you know," said Mrs. Coldstream.

Maha began in a half-chanting tone the following legend,* to which, as she went on, her lady listened not only with curiosity, but with great pleasure and surprise:

---

* The legend is copied almost word for word from a most interesting work which I procured from Calcutta, "The Karen Apostle, or Memoir of Ko Thah Byu," by the Rev. Francis Mason, D.D., missionary to the Karens. I am indebted to this work for the information contained in this story regarding a very remarkable race, as well as regarding the singular man who is the subject of the memoir.

"God created man. And of what did He create man? He created man at first from earth. The creation of man was finished. He created a woman. How did He create a woman? He took a rib out of the man and created again a woman. The creation of woman was finished."

"Why, this is just what is written in the Bible!" cried Io. "Who taught you to read the holy Book?"

"We had no books; we knew nothing. It was like that," said Maha in her natural tone, pointing to a ladder which was leaning against a pillar in the veranda. Maha rose, went to the spot, placed her hand on the ground, and said, "This is Maha;" then touching the first rung, "this father;" the second, "this father's father; up, up, fathers and fathers—no count. I don't know who was the top one—that father long, long way off, perhaps right up in the clouds."

"In the cloud of antiquity indeed," thought Io. "I must hear more of this legend. Come back here, Maha; sing me the rest of your song."

Maha obeyed at once, resumed her place at Io's feet, and with an occasional glance at the picture beside her, went on in the same chanting tone :—

"Father God said, ' My son and daughter, your Father will make and give you a garden. In the garden are seven different kinds of trees bearing seven different kinds of fruit; among the seven one is not good to eat. Eat not of its fruit; if you eat you will become old and will die: eat not. All I have created I give to you. Eat and drink with care. Once in seven days I will visit you. All I have commanded you, observe and do. Forget me not. Pray to me every morning and night.'"

"Every *seven* days!" thought Io to herself. "Have we amongst these poor natives a trace of the institution of the Sabbath, when man should specially meet his God?—Go on, my child," she said aloud.

"I shall have to tell you of a very bad king," said Maha; "that is Ku-plau [*the deceiver*], but some call him Yaw-kaw [*the neck-trodden*]." It was not till afterwards that Io learned the meaning of these strangely appropriate titles given to the enemy of man. We shall change them to the name of Satan, as being more familiar to English readers.

"Afterwards Satan came and said, 'Why are you here?'—'Our Father God put us here,' they replied.— 'What do you eat here?' Satan inquired.—'Our Father God created food and drink for us, food without end.'— Satan said, 'Show me your food.' And they went, with Satan following behind them, to show him. On arriving at the garden, they showed him the fruits, saying, 'This is sweet, this is sour, this is bitter, this is sharp [astringent], this is savoury, this is fiery; but this tree, we know not whether it is sour or sweet. Our Father God said to us, "Eat not of the fruit of this tree; if you eat you will die." We eat not, and do not know whether it be sour or sweet.'"

As she sang Maha touched the fruit which appeared on the tree in the picture, evidently connecting it with that in her legend.

"And what did Satan say to the man and woman?" asked Io.

"Very bad words," answered the girl, and she then went on with her chant:—

"Satan replied, 'The heart of your Father God is not with you. This is the richest and sweetest; it is richer than the others, sweeter than the others. And not merely richer and sweeter, but if you eat it you will possess miraculous powers: you will be able to ascend into heaven and descend into the earth; you will be able to fly. The heart of your God is not with you. The desirable thing he has not given you. I love you, and tell you the whole. Your Father God does not love you; he did not tell you the whole. If you do not believe me, do not eat it. Let each one eat carefully a single fruit, then you will know.' The man replied, 'Our Father God said to us, "Eat not the fruit of this tree," and we eat not.' Thus saying he rose up and went away."

"How wonderfully this legend accords with what St. Paul reveals to us!" thought Io. "'*Adam was not deceived, but the woman being deceived was in the transgression.*'"

"Is the sahiba tired of my song?" asked Maha.

"Oh no; I like extremely to hear it," was Mrs. Coldstream's reply.

Again rose the soft Karen chant :—

" But the woman listened to Satan, and thinking what he said was rather proper, remained. Satan deceived her completely, and she said to him, ' If we eat, shall we indeed be able to fly ? '—' My son and daughter,' said Satan, ' I persuade you because I love you.' The woman took of the fruit and ate. Satan laughing said, ' My daughter, you listen to me well ; now go, give the fruit to your husband and say to him, " I have eaten the fruit ; it is exceedingly rich." If he does not eat, deceive him that he may eat.' The woman, doing as Satan told her, went and coaxed her husband, till she won him over to her own mind, and he took the fruit from the hand of his wife and ate. When he had eaten, she went to Satan and said, ' My husband has eaten the fruit.' On hearing that he laughed exceedingly, and said, ' Now you have listened to me ; very good, my son and daughter.' "

" Is there any more ? " inquired Io, as Maha paused.

" A great deal more, but I did not learn to the end. I can sing what I remember."

" The day after they had eaten, early in the morning God visited them ; but they did not, as they had been wont to do, follow Him with praises. He approached them and said, ' Why have you eaten of the fruit of the tree that I commanded you not to eat ? ' They did not dare to reply, and God cursed them. ' Now you have not observed what I commanded you,' He said. ' The fruit that is not good to eat I told you not to eat; but you have not listened, and have eaten, therefore you shall become old, you shall be sick, you shall die.'"

"That is all that I know well," said Maha; "but father told me how Satan taught the man and woman to worship demons and sacrifice pigs. Our first old father forbade his children and grandchildren to do such bad things."

"How wonderful is this legend!" thought Io; "it describes the Fall far more naturally than our great Milton ever did. One could fancy that in exactly such words Eve told the sad story to her two little boys, Cain and Abel." Then the lady said aloud, "Did your great old father tell you anything of the Flood?"

"I don't know much about that, only very little," replied Maha. "There is one song something like this: 'It thundered; tempests followed; it rained three days and three nights, and the waters covered all the mountains.' I did not like that story so well as that of the woman and man."

Io asked a few more questions, but found Maha utterly ignorant of anything else contained in the Scriptures, except some dim tradition of men separating because they did not love each other. "Their language became different," said the girl, resuming her chanting tone, "and they became enemies to each other and fought."

Io kissed her little pupil, and sent her to play with a kitten. "It is I, not Maha, who have been the learner to-day," thought the lady.

CHAPTER VI.

MODERN THEORIES.

On that day the dinner of the Coldstreams, partaken of an hour or two before sunset, was shared by the chaplain and the doctor. Conversation flowed freely before the party sat down to the meal, Pinfold and Thud, as usual, taking a prominent part; but when the actual business of eating commenced, the two, being the most busily engaged with their knives and forks, became the most silent of those at the table. During the latter part of the social meal Io gave a rather full account of the traditions embodied in the song of the young Karen. She was listened to with an amount of interest varying with the different characters of those who heard her.

"This is most curious, most interesting," observed Coldstream. "To have such a full, independent account of the Fall is such a confirmation of the record contained in the book of Genesis as may well silence infidel objections."

"I don't see that," quoth pragmatical Thud, speaking

with his mouth full of pudding. "Of course these Karens got that story of theirs from Christians."

"Pardon me," said Mr. Lawrence politely; "the tradition of the Fall, and a good many others, existed before a Christian had set his foot in Burmah, Siam, or Pegu."

"I found that Maha knows nothing at all about our Saviour," observed Io, "and Christians would assuredly have spoken of Him."

Thud was not easily put down. "Then the Karens got their old stories from Jews," he said authoritatively. "Jews are always wandering about, and turning up in every country under the sun."

"Permit me again to correct you," said the chaplain. "I happen to have made some researches amongst Karen traditions, and I find that they do not contain the slightest allusion to either Abraham or Moses. This shows that the ancestor whose accounts they rehearse must have lived at a yet more remote period. No son of Abraham would have omitted all mention of the father of the faithful, or of the great lawgiver Moses. The traditions cannot have come from the Jews."

Thud was not yet beaten from his ground. "The traditions came from Jews who were not descended from Abraham," he boldly asserted.

The clergyman and Oscar exchanged glances; Io smiled; Dr. Pinfold burst into a roar of laughter. "You're a rare scholar, you are," he exclaimed to Thud.

" I'm glad that you've found that out at last," said Thud with perfect gravity, as if he had received a well-merited compliment. This misapprehension of the doctor's playful satire made Pinfold throw himself back in his chair with a louder explosion of mirth than the first.

" Thucydides Thorn, if I die of apoplexy from a fit of laughing, my death will lie at your door!" cried the doctor as soon as he had recovered some amount of gravity. He pushed back his chair and rose from the table. " Excuse me, Io. I must be off to a patient; I've a leg to cut off while the daylight lasts.—Mr. Coldstream, look after that sage brother-in-law of yours; if you don't get him into regular harness quickly, he'll die of theories on the brain." As Dr. Pinfold walked along the veranda he was heard laughing to himself still, though the words which he muttered did not reach their subject—" O Thucydides Thorn, thou art indeed an incomparable owl!"

" Dr. Pinfold gives sound advice, Thud," said Oscar; " it is high time that you should be harnessed to regular work. I am afraid that you have not even begun to study the language."

" Oh! no need to study it; I'll drink it in," replied Thud, with sublime indifference to anything like reproof. " I've a theory that language floats about in the air in invisible globules, like cholera or small-pox. We don't set babies to learn grammar or idioms; they catch them exactly as they catch measles."

"It is a pity that Dr. Pinfold is not here to benefit by your medical theory," said Io playfully.

"Dr. Pinfold is a man of very dull wit; he cannot take my theories in," said the learned Thud. "I don't like a fellow who is always cutting stupid jokes: when he wishes to laugh at nothing he laughs at me."

"Surely you do not reckon yourself *nothing*," observed Io.

Thud did not see the point of the observation, so went on with his explanation of the nature of speech. "My theory about the existence of a variety of languages is this,"——the head of the speaker inclined to its position of deep thought as he went on after a pause,—— "every country has its peculiar language, just as it has its peculiar *fauna* and *flora :* we don't meet with alligators in Oxford Street, or gather buttercups at the North Pole. When tribes of ancient times wandered to India, Japan, or England, they gradually, by absorbing air-globules in each region, breathed them out again in various tongues."

The chaplain slightly raised his eye-brows in surprise on hearing notions so original propounded in so solemn a manner.

Io observed, "We have a very different reason for the confusion of tongues given in the Bible."

"Oh, the Bible is an antiquated book," said the owl; "the present enlightened age demands fresh theories and ideas."

" Boy!" exclaimed Oscar Coldstream sternly, " take off the shoes of thy folly when treading on holy ground."

Even Thud looked somewhat startled at his brother-in-law's unexpected rebuke. The soul of Io was quivering with joy, as when the chalice of the white water-lily trembles in the soft south breeze. Her joy was not on account of Thud's receiving a well-earned reproof, though she thought that it might do him good; it was because her husband had been able and willing to give it. Oscar, since his illness, had appeared so crushed that he had almost lost not only his spirits but his spirit. Even Thud had never roused him to a display of indignation till now.

" That flash of anger was just like the gleam of lightning which tells us that longed-for rain is coming !" thought the hopeful young wife. " Oscar, my darling, looked almost like his former self for a moment; and he spoke in defence of God's Word. Oh, all will be well yet; we shall be so happy again !"

Thud was by no means so well pleased as his sister. To be called a boy, and reprimanded for folly, was more than the poor owl could bear. " I am going out," he said sulkily, rising and moving towards the door, but not before providently filling one of his hands with almonds and raisins from the dish before him.

" Stay," said Oscar in a milder tone : " I want to come to a clear understanding with you, Thud, about this matter of work ; for I am sure that Dr. Pinfold is right

in saying that you should now be put into harness, and
do something to gain your own living. I am willing,
as far as possible, to indulge your natural tastes and
inclination. For what kind of employment do you
think yourself most fit ?"

" I should fit a good many," replied Thud, " but the
mischief is that they do not fit me."

" What do you think would suit you ?" asked Oscar.

Thud reflected for a few moments, and then sententiously replied, " I should like the charge of an elephant-
stud."

" There is no elephant-stud in Moulmein," observed
Oscar Coldstream.

" I've seen elephants here," said Thucydides Thorn.

" I think that the rajah has three," observed the
chaplain.

" I know of no other here but the one employed at
the wharf."

" And why should you wish to have charge of elephants, Thud ?" asked Io smiling.

" I wish it because I want to substantiate a theory
which I have formed about the proboscis of the elephant," said Thud, with his air of most profound reflection. " I believe that the proboscis is but an elongated
snout, developed and gradually lengthened by cultivation and civilization—or rather, I may say, by practical
science."

" O Thud, Thud, you are joking !" cried Io.

"I am not joking at all; I scorn jokes!" said Thucydides Thorn. "You women understand nothing about development. Man can alter the shapes of living organizations to an indefinite extent. Look at China: did nature form the tiny feet of its women? See how English ladies can gradually, by tight-lacing, alter their figures till they resemble wasps. I tell you, science can work unimagined wonders. Man saw that elephants would be far more useful creatures if possessing something like a hand, something that could hold and pull —not a mere snout that could only grub in the ground. Gradually, slowly no doubt, the transformation was effected; I will make it my business to find out in what way."

"How is your theory to be reconciled with the fact that the wild elephant possesses a proboscis?" asked Mr. Lawrence with a smile.

"I deny the fact," said Thud. "I believe the elephant to be only a large species of a highly-developed pig, and that the wild one has only a good long snout."

"You can easily test your theory," observed the chaplain, "for one of the elephants of the rajah is quite untamed; it was caught in the jungle only last week."

"I'll be off and see it at once," said Thud, moving more quickly than he usually did, for he desired no repetition of the conversation regarding putting him into harness.

"I shall send the boy to the warehouse to-morrow

morning," said Oscar Coldstream. "I will place him under my clerk Smith, appoint Thud a certain task to perform before dinner-time, and let him understand that he is not expected back here until the task is finished."

"I rather pity Smith," thought the chaplain; "it is no easy task to bring such a born philosopher to submit to being harnessed."

CHAPTER VII.

EXPECTED AND WELCOMED.

THE Coldstreams and their guest now adjourned into the veranda to enjoy the evening air, and the golden glow on foliage and flower which gives such a charm to the sunset hour in the East. Io brought out her work; she was knitting a delicate shawl for her mother. The young matron felt tranquilly happy. She was much pleased to see the friendship which appeared to be already growing up between her husband and the fair-haired, gentle and earnest chaplain.

"It is just what Oscar needed," thought Io, as her fingers plied the ivory needles, whilst her eyes rested on the two gentlemen conversing together. "My husband required a brother-like, pious friend with whom to speak freely on religious subjects—one whose pleasant society may rouse him at last from his mysterious sadness. Mr. Lawrence will be to Oscar in spiritual things what dear old Dr. Pinny will be in matters relating to health. My beloved one will gradually—oh, may Heaven grant it!—recover his natural tone of mind. I shall take care to invite the good chaplain very often to the house. I like his quiet, unobtrusive manner; he is just the person to win the confidence of my husband."

The conversation in the veranda chiefly related to the curious traditions existing amongst the Karens. Mark Lawrence had made them his study, and they had beguiled many an hour that might otherwise have been sad and lonely. The young chaplain had hitherto met with no kindred spirit in the limited society of Moulmein. Full of earnest devotion himself, and a warm sympathizer in the missionary cause, Mark had been discouraged by the difficulty of imbuing others with his own zeal; it was like dragging a heavy load up a hill. The easy-going worldliness of the doctor, the carelessness of Pogson, the stolidity of Cottle, the vulgar loquacity of his wife, made Mark often sadly contrast his position in Moulmein with the happy life which he had led in England in a rural parish where he had almost as many friends as hearers, and where he was a member of a large family circle. Now and then the chaplain had met with missionaries whose names are still honoured and whose work still flourishes. Those days had been red-letter days to Mark Lawrence; but they had been "few and far between"—little oases in a dull, sandy plain. Now, in the accomplished, highly-educated young merchant who had come to reside in Moulmein, the chaplain thought that he had found a real friend—one who would join with him in every labour of love.

"You were much struck, I saw at the tradition of the Fall," said Mr. Lawrence to Oscar; "but still more curious, at least to my mind, are the prophecies which amongst the Karens have been handed down from father to son during ages which no one is able to count."

"What kind of prophecies?" asked Oscar.

"Mysterious foretellings of both the first and second Advent of our Lord," was the reply,—"foretellings which force us on to the conclusion that the ancient ancestor of this singular race must have been a kind of post-diluvian Enoch, inspired by the Spirit of Truth."

"You greatly raise my curiosity," said Oscar. "Can you remember any of these remarkable predictions?"

"Hear the following, which I have committed to memory as well as written down," replied Mr. Lawrence. "What I am about to repeat seems clearly to relate to a Divine Being appearing in great humility on earth:— 'Before God comes, Satan will come deceiving men; but follow him not, children and grandchildren. After Satan will come One with scarcely clothes enough to cover Him. Follow Him; that one is God. When God comes, He will take the appearance of the poorest of men, and will dress in rags. Follow Him!'"

"Oh, is it not as if the ancient sage had caught the sound of the Saviour's then unuttered words—*Follow Me!*" exclaimed Io.

"*The poorest of men,*" repeated Oscar meditatively; "He who had not where to lay His head!"

"But you said that there is a prophecy of the second Advent also," cried Io.   "If you can remember it, pray repeat it."

"The ancient prophet bursts into a triumphant song which has a true Advent ring about it," said the chaplain; and with animation he repeated a translation of the Karen poem :—

> "God comes down, comes down,
>   God descends, descends ;
>   He comes—blowing a trumpet :
> Blowing He gathers men, like the flowers of the areca,
> Sounding He gathers people, like the flowers of the areca ;
>   The glittering, the angels of Heaven,
>   The dazzling, the angels of Heaven,
> The great trumpet that God comes blowing,
> The great one that strikes the golden harp."

"That is glorious !" exclaimed Io, with kindling eyes. "We might set that translation to music and sing it in church."

"Such traditions must have wonderfully prepared the way for Christian missionaries," observed Oscar.

"They did indeed," replied the chaplain.   "The Word of God was received and welcomed too; for there was a prophecy that something was coming which would affect the destiny of the Karen race.   This curious prophecy runs thus : 'Children and grandchildren, if the thing come by land, weep; if by water, laugh.   It will not come in our days, but it will in yours.'"

"The English came by water !" exclaimed Io.

" Yes; and they came bringing the **Word of Life.** The once down-trodden Karens joyously **sang :—**

> ' **The sons of God,** the white foreigners,
> **Dress in shining black** and shining white ;
> The sons of God, the white foreigners,
> Obtained the words of **God.'**

The gospel," continued **the chaplain,** " has **made rapid progress** amongst **the Karens,** and the work, **as far as I** know, seems to **be thorough and** deep."

"I shall take **double pleasure in teaching my little** Maha now," observed Io. " I shall **not regard her as** one of a savage **race, but as the descendant of some** ancient mysterious **prophet who, like Enoch, walked with God."**

CHAPTER VIII.

A REFUSAL.

THE conversation was here interrupted by the return of Thucydides Thorn, who came hastily into the veranda. It needed a good deal to disturb the calm self-assurance which his round, heavy countenance habitually showed, but he now looked rather pale and excited.

"What is the matter, Thud?" cried Io. "Has the rajah's wild elephant being playing on you any prank?"

"I have an idea that we are going to have a rising of the blacks," said Thud, in a very serious tone. "Passing through the bazaar, I heard a furious rebel haranguing the mob, who listened open-mouthed while he preached rebellion."

"How do you know that he preached rebellion?" asked Oscar.

"I could tell it by his flashing eyes and his eager speech. Crowds gathered round him, fascinated by his wild gestures. Take my word for it, that man was inciting the niggers to cut all our throats."

"What sort of a man was the orator in appearance ?" asked Lawrence, looking rather interested than alarmed.

"He is not young—about fifty or sixty years old," was the reply; "he was just a common native."

"A very *uncommon* native," said Mr. Lawrence, "if you have seen, as I have reason to suppose, the Karen apostle, Ko Thah Byu. I have been expecting him to pass through Moulmein, and am heartily glad that he has come. I shall feel my house honoured if that Karen evangelist sleep to-night under my roof."

"He does not look as if he were much accustomed to sleep under roofs," observed Thud. "I daresay that the beggar has seldom had anything better than a tree over his head."

"You judge correctly," said Mr. Lawrence. "Ko Thah Byu was originally but a village boy, and he was afterwards the servant of Mr. Hough, and then of a native Christian."

"I daresay that he was a bad servant," observed Thud, who was rather annoyed at his dangerous rebel and incendiary proving to be nothing but a harmless preacher.

"Again you are right, Mr. Thorn," said the chaplain: "the now devoted Christian was, before his conversion, a very bad servant and a very bad man. But when Ko Thah Byu became a believer in Christ, he also gradually became an altered character. If there ever were in this dark land a devoted and successful evangelist, that evangelist is Ko Thah Byu."

"I daresay that he is successful in taking in missionaries," remarked Thud ; "they will find him out to be a hypocrite in the end."

Io saw that both the gentlemen looked annoyed at the idle remark, and she made a diversion in the conversation.

"Thud, you know less of missions and converts than of natural history," she playfully observed. "Tell us the result of your scientific researches to-day. Had the wild elephant a trunk, or a snout according to your new theory ?"

Thud looked sulky but not disconcerted. "*This* one had a proboscis," he reluctantly owned ; "but exceptions prove the rule."

"Oh, own yourself beaten for once !" cried Io.

Thud never owned himself beaten, but to avoid being further pressed he availed himself of the usual resource of the vanquished, and beat a retreat.

"I wish, Mr. Lawrence," said Oscar, "that you would take that boy a little in hand. He does not seem to care for his sister's advice and instruction."

"But no doubt the youth receives religious teaching from yourself," observed Mr. Lawrence.

"No ; I never speak on spiritual subjects," was the grave, almost stern reply, and Oscar rose from his seat as he made it.

The chaplain looked greatly surprised. "I have heard of your taking a lead in religious exercises," he said.

"I never do so now," answered Coldstream in the same constrained tone, looking on the ground as he spoke.

"I hope—I do hope, that you will kindly make an exception in my favour to-morrow," said the young clergyman. "I have a little Saturday meeting; it is but poorly attended, but I trust that a blessing may be granted at last. If you would kindly conduct it to-morrow, some might come to hear you who would not cross the road to listen to me. I own that I speak self-ishly," continued Mr. Lawrence, a slight flush rising to his cheek. "I have long looked forward to the pleasure and privilege of spending one day with Ko Thah Byu— of accompanying him as he goes preaching in the villages around, and listening to the untutored eloquence which has such power with the natives. To-morrow may be my single opportunity of gratifying this long-cherished wish, and the only obstacle to my going is this little Saturday meeting. If you would consent to take it—" Lawrence turned towards Mrs. Coldstream with the intention of asking her to further his request, and was almost startled by seeing her gaze of intense anxiety, as with her eyes riveted on her husband she waited to hear his reply.

"I cannot—I will not speak on the subject of religion," said Oscar, still looking on the ground.

"But, dear friend—let me call you so," pleaded the chaplain—"I have heard of the power of your addresses. In refusing to speak for the Master may you not be burying a talent, may you not be hiding a light?"

Then Oscar raised his eyes to meet the gaze of Mark Lawrence. The gloomy expression in them was such as the chaplain could never forget, or the bitterness of the tone in which Coldstream replied to his friend's remonstrance: "Would you think it meet to take an unrinsed glass from a publican's counter and use it as a chalice?" Then, without waiting for a reply, Oscar turned on his heel and strode out of the veranda into the garden beyond.

"Is the poor fellow insane?" thought the chaplain.

"O Mr. Lawrence, Mr. Lawrence, do not let this make you misjudge my husband!" exclaimed Io in bitter distress; "he is one of the best—yes, one of the most religious of men!" The poor lady was unconsciously wringing her hands as she spoke.

"I would not willingly misjudge any one," said the chaplain gently, "especially one for whom I already feel respect and regard."

"You cannot respect him too much," said the wife; "I cannot think why my husband should speak as he did." Io could not bear to tell the chaplain what she had concealed from the doctor, of that which was the bitterest trial which she had had to endure in her married life. Oscar had refused to conduct even family prayer, though he daily read the Bible to Thud and herself. Coldstream was willing that his wife should pray; he never restrained her devotions either by look or word; but he seemed to be kept back by some invisible and incomprehensible barrier from audibly joining in them himself.

There was a painful pause for several minutes, which was broken by Mr. Lawrence. The chaplain had risen to take his leave, but was arrested by a thought which had just occurred to his mind.

"Perhaps it is Mr. Coldstream's very great conscientiousness, his shrinking from anything approaching to hypocrisy, that makes him act in this way," suggested the clergyman.

"You think so?" asked Io anxiously, like one catching at a straw of hope. "All seems to me so dark."

"Perhaps I may throw a little gleam of light on the cause of Mr. Coldstream's depression," said the pitying chaplain. "I believe that early this year he returned to England in the *Argus*, in which ship Mr. Pogson was his fellow-passenger. May I ask whether your husband has spoken much regarding that voyage?"

"He has never said a word to me about it," was Io's reply; "I never even heard the name of Mr. Pogson."

"I am not surprised at that," observed Mr. Lawrence; "there would be little in common between Mr. Coldstream and Pogson. The young man holds a small Government appointment, and this year, like your husband, paid a short visit to England, from whence he returned a few weeks ago. Pogson told me of another passenger in the *Argus*, a Mr. Mace, whom I happen to know. Mr. Mace is a clever man, but unhappily quite a freethinker. Pogson informed me that Mr. Mace used often to discuss religious questions with Mr. Coldstream."

"My husband would never be overcome in argument by a freethinker," exclaimed the young wife.

"Probably not," was the chaplain's reply; "but infidels fight with poisoned weapons, and even a scratch, so to speak, on a mind so delicately conscientious as that of your husband would be likely to fester and cause acute pain."

"It would indeed," said Io.

"Had Mr. Coldstream any doubt, however slight, on a point regarding Christian doctrine, he might make it a point of honour, even of conscience, not to make much profession of piety until that doubt should quite disappear."

"Oh, thank you, bless you for that word!" exclaimed Io. "Then our trouble must be short-lived, for every doubt will—must disappear in the light of the truth, and my husband will again serve God with gladness, and come into His presence with thanksgiving, as in the happy old times. If any evil has been put into Oscar's mind, you will by God's help remove it; you will speak to my husband on religion, on the evidences of our holy faith."

"I shall try to do so," said the chaplain, "but perhaps not just at once. A little time may— But here comes your husband again," continued Mark Lawrence, looking towards a tall figure that was approaching through the deepening twilight.

Oscar Coldstream went up straight to his guest. " Mr. Lawrence," he said, " I must ask your forgiveness for having left you so abruptly." The gentlemen exchanged a kindly grasp of the hand, and then Oscar went on, " You touched a sensitive point; may I request you kindly never to broach that subject again ? "

Mark Lawrence made no promise, but after shaking Mrs. Coldstream's hand, silently took his leave.

CHAPTER IX.

QUIET CONVERSE.

"My first Sabbath in this land of the East!" thought Io, as her eyes first unclosed on Sunday morning. "This is a Communion Sabbath too. Oh, shall I to-day be granted the priceless blessing, which I have not enjoyed since my marriage, of having my heart's beloved at my side when I approach the Lord's table? May my Oscar, as well as his wife, make this a day of new consecration to any work which the Master may give us to do! May we both begin a closer 'walk with God,' and find happiness in the consciousness of His abiding presence!"

Such were Io's hopes; her fears need not be recorded.

The Coldstreams preferred walking to church, though Io was to return in a palanquin to avoid the heat of the sun as the day advanced. Thud sauntered along beside his sister.

"I shall like to hear the chaplain preach," observed Io.

"I don't expect much from that pale little man, though I daresay he's a good sort of fellow," said Thud in a patronizing way. "I don't think he'll give us anything new."

"In religion the old things are best," remarked Io. "So in nature what we have had longest we value most; indeed, speaking of such things, 'old' is not the right word. The sun, moon, stars, the breezes, the glorious sea, never grow old. Even of the flowers I like to think that we see the very same kind of blossoms that bloomed under the eye of Eve."

"But 'the trail of the serpent is over them all,'" murmured Oscar under his breath.

"Not all—oh, not all!" exclaimed Io, catching the figurative meaning of Moore's mournful line. "Such love as ours is a pure fragrant flower of Eden—resembling this." Io plucked a very beautiful rose from a bush; for in southern climes even November and December have their roses.

"That rose has a worm in it," said Thud; "don't you see the little round hole in the petals?"

"You are quick-sighted to see the blemish in the beautiful," observed Oscar Coldstream.

"Oh yes, I am pretty quick-sighted," said Thucydides Thorn with self-satisfaction.

The church was at no very great distance. The congregation was small, but to Io there was peaceful joy in finding herself again in a place of worship, and hearing in her native tongue dear familiar words of prayer. She sang God's praises with heart and soul, though the music was hardly such as would have pleased a critical ear, and the rich, deep voice which used

formerly to blend with hers was silent now. Only once
did Oscar join in a single verse, "From lowest depths
of woe," and then he was silent again. Oscar knelt
silently during the prayers, save that in a low tone he
repeated the first responses in the Litany ; in the Thanksgiving Io could not catch the sound of his voice.

It has been mentioned that the Moulmein congregation
was a small one ; at the Communion Service it became
smaller still. Io noticed with a pang that Oscar left
her side and walked out of the church before that part
of the service began. Thud had departed almost before
the blessing was pronounced. He did not walk home
with Oscar, but joined young Pogson, whose society was
more congenial to the lad.

"I say, it must be jolly to you to have a comfortable
nest to roost in, with such a pretty sister to keep house,
and such a gay, lively companion as Coldstream, instead
of having to elbow your way through the world like
me," observed Pogson, who was lighting a cigar.

"Gay—lively!" echoed Thud with as much surprise
as his heavy countenance could express. "Why, Oscar's
as grave as judge, jury, and criminal all put together!
—Give me a cigar, will you?" Thud thought it a
dignified thing to smoke.

"Coldstream must be wonderfully changed then since
his marriage," quoth Pogson. "I thought that he looked
very grave, but he always was solemn in church."

"I've a theory that marriage does make men grave

and solemn," said Thud. "Marriage alters them altogether. I never mean to marry, or let any girl have a
chance of altering me."

"You think that no alteration could be an improvement," said Pogson with a smile. The sarcasm was lost
on Thucydides Thorn; he seldom understood when he
was the object of satire.

Joy and sorrow, hope and fear, were commingled in
the heart of Io Coldstream as she returned in her
palanquin to her new home. The service in church had
refreshed her spirit; it was sweet to the young Christian
to try to lay her burden down at the Saviour's feet. But
she still felt where the burden had chafed; there was
not perfect repose in her soul. Often and often did Io
review in her mind her conversation with the chaplain
on the subject of Oscar's depression.

"Very holy men have before now had spiritual difficulties and mental trials," reflected Io. "Does not Bunyan represent even his Christian and Hopeful in Doubt-
ing Castle under the tyranny of Giant Despair? They
indeed had strayed from the narrow path. I cannot
think that Oscar has ever thus strayed, but yet he may
have his giant to fight. Christian had the key of
promise in his bosom, and so, I am sure, has my husband.
I will be Oscar's Hopeful, and we will escape together.
No doubts can for long imprison those whom the truth
has set free."

Io found Oscar sitting in the veranda, a volume of
(180)   6

Herbert's poems in his hand, but he did not appear to be reading. Mr. Coldstream rose when the palanquin was set down by the bearers, and helped his wife out of the conveyance. He then brought another chair from the house, and he and Io sat down together. The lady wished to bring on conversation on some religious subject, and naturally recurred to the chaplain's sermon, the first which the Coldstreams had heard from his lips.

"Did you not think the preacher's words very comforting?" said Io after a pause, feeling that she must be the first to break the silence.

"Searching, incisive," was the reply.

"To what part do you allude, dear Oscar? The address was all upon following the Lord and receiving His blessing."

"A conditional blessing," said Oscar.

"Surely not, dearest. Our salvation is free; Mr. Lawrence pressed that point on us," observed Io Coldstream.

"Was there nothing in the sermon about cutting off the right hand and plucking out the right eye?" asked her husband.

"That is but a figure of speech."

"A figure, I grant you, but conveying a fact. It is too much the way with men to take all that is pleasant and soothing in Scripture and to leave out the sterner truths. That figure does imply the surrender, at any cost, of what is dear as a hand or an eye."

There was rather a prolonged silence ; then Io lovingly laid her hand on her husband's arm, and softly said, " Do you not think that the greatest trial which we can ever be called on to bear is to lose one whom we love ? "

" No ; there is a heavier cross even than that," muttered Oscar, as if speaking to himself rather than to his young wife.

Io felt a little perplexed, and even hurt ; but she ventured not to ask for any explanation of words so strange. She was pleased to see Mr. Lawrence at a little distance approaching the house.

" I will leave him and my husband to have a quiet talk together," thought Mrs. Coldstream. Rising, and saying that she had not yet given Maha her Sunday lesson, Io glided into the house.

During his walk to the dwelling of the Coldstreams Mark's soul had been engaged in fervent prayer. The Saturday evening had been chiefly devoted to searching learned books, written for the special purpose of refuting infidel views and clearing up doubts on difficult doctrines.

Oscar received his visitor with his usual courtesy, and Mark was invited to occupy the seat which Io had quitted.

The chaplain had revolved in his mind how he could best lead the conversation with his friend to the point which he had in his view. He must not wound, he must not startle, above all he must not offend. After a few insignificant observations, which with our shy nation seem indispensable as a shoe-horn to real conversation, Mr. Lawrence observed, "You went home, I believe, in the *Argus?*"

Coldstream assented by a slight movement of the head.

"You must have met on board a passenger of the name of John Mace?"

There was again the mute sign of assent.

"May I ask what you thought of him?" inquired the chaplain.

"I thought him intelligent and gentlemanly," replied Oscar, "but he had imbibed some very erroneous views."

"I know it—I know it," said Mark Lawrence. "Mr. Mace made no secret of them here. Did you ever enter into conversation with him on religious subjects?"

"Very often," was the quiet reply.

Mark felt that he was drawing near to his point. "May I ask what impression Mr. Mace made on your mind?" said the chaplain.

"At first a painful impression; but Mace was candid, and open to conviction. He came on board the *Argus* an infidel; he left it, I have good reason to hope, a truly converted man."

"Is it possible!" exclaimed the clergyman joyfully. "And you—*you* were the happy instrument of his conversion?"

Oscar's face did not reflect the look of pleasure on that of his friend. "God sometimes uses strange instruments," was his only reply.

" But this is a thing to be a joy to you all your life !" exclaimed Mark. " You have then never had doubts yourself ? "

" Any difficulties which suggested themselves to my mind in my younger days were but as thin vapours which rather clothe a rock than hide it. They only led me to examine more closely, and so believe more firmly. I could always see the rock behind the vapour, and I long since planted my feet firmly upon it."

" Thank God ! thank God !" was Mark's inward ejaculation. " But if it be no doubt on speculative religion that oppresses my poor friend, what cause can there be for his deep-rooted sadness ? Coldstream is happily married ; he has good social position, competence, and high reputation ; why should he be as one oppressed by a secret grief ? "

Again came the painful suspicion, " Can this be melancholy madness ? "

CHAPTER X

"WHERE have you been, Thud?" inquired Io, as, a few hours after her return from church, her brother sauntered into the drawing-room, smelling of tobacco, and with his thumbs in his waistcoat pockets.

"I've had a good chat and smoke with Pogson," replied Thud, throwing himself on the sofa; "and as talking and tobacco make one dry, we had something to wet our whistles. He's no water-drinker, like Oscar."

"I do not think that Pogson is a good companion for you, Thud," said Io.

"That's little you know," was the rude reply. Thud could treat his sister as he liked when her husband was absent.

"What did you talk about?" inquired Io.

"Oh, a lot of things, scientific and other; but Pogson is not scientific. He only laughed at my theory of there being animalcula in fire, as well as in water and air. He said I'd burn my fingers in trying to find them, though it goes to reason that what is found in three elements is sure to be in the fourth, though philosophers have not yet found them out."

"I do not wonder at Pogson's not caring for such theories," said Io. "Perhaps your search for animalcula in the candle will result in the grand discovery of some poor moths who have singed off their wings in the flame."

"We talked of other matters too, not scientific," said Thud, who was busying himself in picking out threads from the fringe of a handsome cushion. "Pogson told me a great deal about his voyage in the *Argus*. You would have liked that, for he spoke so much about Oscar."

"What did he say of my husband?" asked Io, roused to interest.

"Oh! that he was very sociable and very amusing; sang songs and told anecdotes without end, except when he walked up and down the deck, holding grave discourse with a man called Mace. During the latter part of the voyage, however, Oscar was much taken up with reading poetry, and carrying about chairs for, and playing the agreeable to, a handsome widow whom they picked up at Malta."

"What widow?" asked Io Coldstream.

"One whose husband had died at Malta, and who took the opportunity of returning home in the *Argus*. Pogson says that she was a former friend of Oscar, a very particular friend, probably before her marriage.

Anyways, Mrs. Mortimer—that's her name—told Pogson that she has a picture in which she and Oscar are taken together, she sitting on a mossy bank, and Oscar offering her a rose."

"Thud, you talk nonsense!" exclaimed Io indignantly. Her cheek was flushed and burning, but her hands trembled as if with cold.

"I never talk nonsense," said Thud majestically, "and I have no reason to think that Pogson does so either. The widow's Christian name is Adelaide, for she said that hers is the same as the Queen's. She usually addressed Oscar by his Christian name, in quite a familiar way. He used to take great care of her; she was clearly a very particular friend indeed. You had better ask Oscar about her."

Io felt as if her heart had suddenly become like a stone; but she reproached herself indignantly for giving one moment's credit to such idle gossip. She would not let Thud see that he had inflicted a pang; but had his thick fingers not been so engaged in spoiling the fringe, had he glanced up for a moment, even Thud would have seen in his sister's face the annoyance caused by his words.

"I wish that you would leave that cushion alone," said Io sharply. It was to hide her agitation under the semblance of anger.

"You are as cross as a crustacean to-day," said Thud, throwing the cushion away. "I don't see the use of your church-going, if you come back in such a bad temper ;" and so saying, he quitted the room.

"How foolish, how absurd, how wrong in me to think anything of such talk!" said Io to herself. "My dear husband is always courteous, to a widow he would be doubly so; as for what that silly fellow said about the picture, I would not credit it for a moment. Adelaide Mortimer!" Io revolved in her mind whether she had ever heard the name from Oscar's lips; but no, she could not recall his having once mentioned to her this very particular friend.

It still wanted an hour to dinner time; that hour might be pleasantly and profitably spent in reading, especially if Io read with Oscar. The lady chose her book, and then went into the veranda to look for her husband. Oscar was not there, but he had left the small volume of Herbert's poems on the chair on which he had been seated during his interview with the chaplain.

"A few of Herbert's quaint verses will be refreshing," thought Io. "I never possessed a copy of his works of my own. What dainty delicate binding!" and the lady took up the pretty volume.

Io opened at the title-page to see who had published the graceful edition. But it was not on title of work or publisher's name that her eyes were riveted now; it was no thought of Herbert that made her cheek, so lately flushed, turn almost as white as the paper on which she looked. Above the printed title was written,

in a delicate feminine hand: *Oscar William Coldstream.
With Adelaide Mortimer's love.*

Io uttered no exclamation, gave no start; she gazed
for several minutes on the inscription, and then de-
liberately closed the volume and laid it down again in
the place from which she had raised it. Io went back
into the house, entered her own room, closed the door
and bolted it, but almost like one who walks in a dream.
Her soul was in a state of wild chaos; it was some time
before she could sufficiently collect her thoughts to draw
any inferences, form any conjectures.

Then, like machinery suddenly put into violent motion,
Io's mind began to work on the few facts from which she
might draw some clue to the cause of the terrible change
in Oscar when he returned to England. He had been
happy when he had embarked, wretched when he landed.
One idea, like wheel within wheel, linked itself with
another, while Io's brain seemed to turn round with the
action of passionate thought.

Had Oscar loved Adelaide before he had even known
of the existence of Io? Had Mrs. Mortimer's marriage
divided her from a former lover by an impassable gulf?
After a bitter disappointment, had Oscar tried to find
solace by winning the love and confidence of an un-
suspecting heart, and asked in marriage a girl to whom
he could but offer an empty casket, from which the
jewel of affection had been stolen away? On arriving
in Malta, had Oscar found the once impassable gulf

bridged over; had the **unexpected** meeting with Adelaide, no longer **as** far removed from him as a star,
revived old memories, **kindled new** hopes? And then
had Oscar remembered with pain **that he had** bound
himself **in honour to marry one** whom he never could
love as he **once had loved?**

Io could not have put such **ideas into words, but they**
were working, **and** tearing her heart **as a** machine rends
and wrenches **a human limb** entangled **amongst its**
whirling wheels. **She could hardly reason, but she**
keenly suffered. **Hard** did **Io strive so to collect her**
ideas as to find **out whether her new discovery would**
account for **that** gloom **in her husband which had**
seemed **to her so** mysterious. Oscar had **received no**
letter from **her at** Malta, none **by the Channel** pilot:
had her apparent neglect **caused him pain, or perhaps**
a sense **of** relief? **Had he caught at a hope** that he
might **be** *free?* **What had** prompted **that** strange
question **when they met,** *"Are you glad?"* **Had he**
wished **her to turn away and say "No"?** Oscar was
evidently undergoing some terrible inward struggle, **and**
was suffering **still from its effects. Was it the struggle**
between inclination, love, passion, and a sense of honour,
a feeling of duty? Io remembered, almost **with horror,**
that during the first part **of his illness** Oscar could **not**
endure to have her near him; that he only suffered her
presence **when the** sight **of the** letter **which** Thud **had**
detained **had shown** him the depth **of** the affection

which, as Io now thought in her anguish, he knew that he could never fully return. Oscar had not even asked that a wedding-day should be fixed, till he found that to break off his engagement would be to leave his betrothed to poverty as well as to distress. Oscar had generously sacrificed himself to save her, preferring honour to happiness, giving pity instead of love! Io literally writhed under such thoughts.

"Oh, why did Oscar not speak out frankly! why did he not tell me that he could not give me a heart which was no longer his own!" exclaimed Io in the bitterness of her anguish. "I would not have upbraided him; I would have set him free; I would have severed the bond between us, had my poor heart been broken too. Oscar should never have stood at the altar to give me that cold, corpse-like hand, or to take vows which are now an intolerable burden to a sensitive conscience like his."

Alas for the woman who lets the scorpion jealousy creep into the shrine of her heart! It brings with it a brood of other reptiles—wounded pride, unreasonable dislike, doubt of the truth of human affection, too often doubt of the love of God. Poor Hopeful was indeed now in the dungeon-keep of the giant. The water-lily that had risen above the waters of trouble now appeared to be withering, dying, from the worm secretly gnawing at its root.

In the midst of her agony of mind Io was loyal to her husband. She did not blame him; he was generous, good, and kind. Oscar was, Io felt, doing his utmost to keep faithfully vows that should never have been made. He was trying by constant, most considerate kindness to make up for the absence of love. What should she do now? She could do nothing but accept the gracious pity which for her had a sting. *Pity!* How Io hated the word, and how she hated herself for so doing! In the morning of that Sabbath day she could not have believed that she could have fallen so far. Io seemed to herself a different being from the young wife who had so peacefully walked to church leaning on the arm of her husband. How some sudden temptation often opens our eyes to our own inconsistency of character, our weakness, worthlessness, and sin! We thought that we were safe and strong, and behold, a perilous fall!

> " Perhaps the angel's slackened hand
>   Hath suffered it, that we may rise,
> And take a firmer, surer stand ;
>   Or trusting less to earthly things,
>   May henceforth learn to use our wings."

Whilst Io was agonizing in her own room, Oscar was in his study, kneeling, with clasped hands, in the attitude of prayer, but the words gasped out were not words of submission. "Any sacrifice but this, any cross but *this!*" was all that burst, as if wrung by extreme mental suffering, from his pale lips.

CHAPTER XI.

A PRESCRIPTION.

As may be imagined, the dinner which was soon after-wards partaken of by the family was anything but a cheerful meal. For the first time Io sat opposite to her husband gloomy and silent, scarcely touching the food before her.

"Are you not well, my love?" asked Oscar anxiously. "I ought not to have suffered you to walk to church in the heat."

"It did me no harm; it was my own will to walk," replied Io coldly.

Oscar gave an uneasy, questioning glance. Io did not choose to meet it. "I don't want his pity," she said to herself.

There was a long, dreary pause, which only Thud filled up by a vigorous onslaught on the mutton. He had almost satisfied his appetite, and was beginning, in nautical phrase, to get his talking-tackle on board, when the circle was joined by Pinfold.

"Ha! ha! happy to catch you just at dinner-time.

I hope our friend Thud has left something for me!" cried the jovial doctor, as he laid down his sun-hat and umbrella, and wiped his heated forehead. Then, advancing to the table, Pinfold greeted his god-daughter in very paternal fashion. The doctor considered himself to be a privileged person, one who need never wait for an invitation, being always certain to find a welcome.

Mr. Coldstream intensely disliked the intrusion, and the vulgar familiarity of his guest. Oscar had been on civil terms with Pinfold during his first sojourn at Moulmein, but intimate he never had been. The two men had nothing in common between them: the mirth of the one had been refined wit, like a sparkle over deep waters; the fun of the other had the coarse scent of the oil-fed torch. But Oscar resolved to show no sign of dislike towards one whom his wife regarded as her oldest friend; Pinfold should always have a seat at the table of her who had sat on his knee when she was a little rosy-cheeked child. Oscar would endure the doctor's society, and not betray, even by a look, that he found that it required some self-command to do so.

"Why, my dear," said Pinfold, addressing himself to Io, "you don't look well; you are losing your roses!"

"I am quite well. Please sit down, dear Dr. Pinny. I am afraid that the meat is a little cold."

"I must come rather earlier next time," said the doctor, taking a seat.—"Well, Thud, what new discoveries have you been making in science?—A little more fat, Coldstream, if you please."

"I've been directing my attention to the moon," said Thud sententiously, laying down the knife and fork which he had been diligently plying.

"No doubt the moon is flattered by the attention shown to her. Ha! ha! ha! I am not surprised at your thoughts being turned in a lunatic direction. How often have you seen the new moon rise in the east?"

"Often," replied Thud, looking surprised at the question.

"Clever dog! you have then seen what no one else ever saw!" cried the doctor.

"You don't mean to say that the moon ever rises in the *west!*" cried Thucydides Thorn, which set the doctor off laughing again. When he had recovered his gravity, Pinfold resumed his questioning.

"May I ask what discoveries you have made in the lunatic direction?"

"I've made no decided discoveries yet," replied Thud; "but a theory is gradually developing itself in my brain."

"Ah! that brain. It will have some day to be put into spirits and deposited in a museum!" cried the doctor.

"I've no objection," said the young philosopher, who was rather gratified by the idea; "but it must be after I'm dead."

This gave the doctor another uproarious fit of mirth, which almost occasioned a choke.

"Now for your theory," he cried, as soon as he had recovered his breath.

"I can't talk whilst you laugh so," said Thud.

"Come, I've had my laugh out; I want to hear your original views regarding our satellite," said Pinfold.

"Some philosophers declare that the moon has no atmosphere," began Thud, as if commencing a lecture.

"That is, I believe, pretty generally acknowledged," observed Coldstream. "Most powerful telescopes have been brought to bear upon the moon, and no trace of atmosphere has been discovered."

"Not on the surface, I grant you," said Thud sententiously. "What I maintain is that the atmosphere is *under* the surface, so that no telescope can reveal it. I have an idea," Thud glanced up towards the ceiling, as if the idea were floating somewhere above the heads of his hearers—"I've a notion that the moon is full of air, something like a balloon, and that as that air expands by the action of heat, or contracts, the moon assumes the shape of the orb or crescent."

Again the doctor gave way to his mirth. "You would make out the queen of night to be a kind of big bladder-ball! O Thucydides Thorn, when will you leave off playing at ninepins! You put up your wooden theories to let us have the fun of knocking them down."

"It is I who knock down old wooden theories like ninepins," said Thud, blinking like an offended owl. "I am aiming after something original and new. We learn by finding out the mistakes of our elders. Every generation stands on the heads of the last."

The doctor threw himself back on his chair, half convulsed with laughter. "A difficult kind of intellectual gymnastics," he cried. "Of course, at the top of the philosophical pyramid will stand—Mr. Thucydides Thorn." The doctor glanced at Io, expecting to see her join in his mirth, but her grave, pale face reflected no spark of amusement.

"I say, Coldstream, you'll have to put your wife under my care," said the doctor abruptly; "she has neither appetite for her food nor spirit for a joke."

"I am a little uneasy about her," began Oscar, but the doctor rather rudely cut him short.

"You'd better be more than a little uneasy; I never saw her look so ill and pale in my life."

"I have a slight headache," said Io, rising. It was very unpleasant to her to have attention called to her looks, so she made an excuse for retiring which was at least a true one. Pinfold followed his god-daughter as far as the door of her room, to put a few questions and feel her pulse. He then returned to the dining-room, where he found Oscar alone, and looking exceedingly anxious. A terrible dread had arisen in the mind of Coldstream that he was to be chastised through the sufferings of his young wife.

"I can't find out that there's anything particular the matter with Io," said Pinfold, resuming his seat; "but she's out of spirits. And no wonder: flowers always lose their colour if kept in the darkness of a cellar. My pretty god-child needs more light, more sunshine, more cheerful society. She—by nature full of fun, the merriest, most lively of girls—cannot keep up her spirits whilst she never sees a smile on the face of her husband."

Pinfold had resolved on getting to the bottom of the mystery of Mr. Coldstream's melancholy; the doctor had often revolved in his mind how to approach so delicate a subject, and now, seeing the evil affecting his favourite's happiness, the old man resolved on throwing false delicacy aside. Coldstream had to endure close questioning, and bore it as he might have done the pain of an operation, only lancet and knife would not have inflicted suffering so acute to a sensitive nature. To Pinfold's questions Oscar returned short, straightforward replies. As he had perceived that the chaplain had suspected him of freethinking, so he was perfectly aware that the doctor doubted his sanity, and Oscar determined to lay that question to rest. No, none of his family had ever been mentally afflicted; he himself had never been in youth subject to depression; he had never been bitten by dog or fox.

"Then why are you so changed—so gloomy?" asked Pinfold. "Any pecuniary trouble? Perhaps you have fallen into debt?"

Coldstream shook his head. "I have neither lent nor borrowed; I have no anxiety connected with money."

"Then what *is* on your mind?" asked the baffled inquisitor.

"That question **hardly lies** within the province of a medical man," said Coldstream rather sternly, for patience had been strained to the utmost point.

Even Pinfold saw that he had gone **too far.** Rising, he concluded the disagreeable interview with a few emphatic injunctions :—

"I'm going to send Io a tonic, but her best tonic would be a more cheerful home. **You** must amuse her and make her happy. **You can do more for** your wife's health, **mark me,** Coldstream, **than the** whole college of physicians can do."

CHAPTER XII.

CONJECTURES.

EARNESTLY did Coldstream strive to impart cheerfulness to his young wife, but he could not give what he himself did not possess. He read aloud to her lively books, brought Shakespeare and Hood for evening amusement; but Hood's jests fell utterly flat, and even Petruchio caused no smile. The doctor recommended horse exercise: the prettiest pony in Moulmein was instantly purchased. Oscar procured flowers of the most rare kind, fruits of the most delicate flavour. Thud enjoyed the fruits, Io languidly admired the flowers; but the rose did not return to the lady's cheek, nor the smile to her lips. At first Oscar's considerate kindness but raised the thought, "How conscientiously my poor husband tries to do his duty, and hide from his wife that he only married her from pity!" Gradually, however, another thought arose, "All this beautiful tenderness cannot be feigned. My Oscar can never deceive."

There was a great deal of gossip in the small society of Moulmein regarding the Coldstreams. Mrs. Cottle, a

vulgar, bustling little woman, declared that she knew
for certain that Mr. Coldstream ill-treated or at least
neglected his wife.   It was clear that they did not
"pull together."   Dr. Pinfold doubted whether the
climate of Moulmein suited the constitution of Io.
Thud, in slow measured tones, as if pronouncing a
medical opinion founded on deep study of the case,
declared that his sister had caught some kind of malady
from that Karen girl who was always dangling at her
heels ; the fact being that almost the sole pleasure which
Io was now able to enjoy was that of tending and teaching the docile and grateful orphan.

The friend who took the most earnest and prayerful
interest in what concerned the Coldstreams was Mark
Lawrence, the chaplain.   He noticed that Io now looked
almost as sad as her husband, and Mark naturally attri-
buted her sorrow to the too evident fact that something
was hiding the light of God's countenance from Oscar
Coldstream.   It was a cause of grief to the wife (of this
Mark felt assured) that lips once eloquent for the Master
were strangely sealed; that a sincere Christian, as the
chaplain believed his friend to be, could not, or would
not, enjoy the child's privilege of approaching his Father's
table.   The more earnest the wife's piety, the deeper
her sorrow if her husband could not participate in its
comfort.

"But the wife takes a wrong way if she seeks to win
a wanderer back by reproaches, even if conveyed but by

sorrowful looks," thought Mark. "I do not believe a word of what Mrs. Cottle says of unkindness on Cold-stream's part, but his manner may **betray** that he is wounded and **hurt.** A small, almost imperceptible **rift** may be widened, a slight injury be **fretted into a sore."**

Such thoughts were on the mind of the pastor as he bent his steps **one day to the** dwelling **of the** Cold-streams. Mark **found the lady in the** veranda, **and** alone.

Io had had **no** opportunity of speaking quietly **with** Mr. Lawrence since he had had that private conversa-tion with her husband which has **been** recorded above. Io had longed **to** know whether **the** chaplain's fears **as** to the **evil** influence of Mr. Mace had been dissipated or confirmed. **A** feeling **of** delicacy prevented Io from asking any question, **but Mark** anticipated her wish. The chaplain had scarcely done **more than** exchanged greetings with the lady, and taken a seat near her, when he entered himself **on the subject which was** uppermost in each mind.

"Mrs. Coldstream," said Mark, "I had done injustice to your husband **when** suspecting, even for **a** moment, that the words **of an infidel** could **have the** slightest effect **on a** mind so clear **and** steady **as his.** Let me repeat **to you** Mr. Coldstream's own words. He said that any difficulties on the subject of Christianity which might have arisen in his mind in his youth had been but as light vapours ; they had **led him** but **to more** close examination of the Rock behind them, and on that Rock he had long since planted his foot."

"Thank God for that!" exclaimed Io.

"You have yet more for which to thank Him," said the chaplain. "Far from Mr. Mace having drawn away your husband from that Rock, the freethinker has been drawn towards it by the Christian, and the result of that intercourse has been the salvation of the infidel's soul."

"Most blessed work!" murmured Io, joyful tears suffusing her eyes.

"I am persuaded," continued Mr. Lawrence, "that it is only some passing cloud that now casts a shadow over my dear friend, and prevents him from being able to enjoy the full privileges of a believer. The cloud will pass, I feel assured that it will pass for ever away, and my friend, himself rejoicing in the light, will again throw himself, heart and soul, into the happy service of his Lord."

"God grant it!" said Io fervently, the tears which had glistened beneath her dark lashes now bedewing her cheeks. "I hope much from your counsel and friendship."

"Nay, let your hope rest on God's mercy and love," said Mark Lawrence, "and hasten the blessing by faith and prayer. You can do far more than I can, Mrs. Coldstream, to restore happiness to your husband."

"What can I do?" asked Io faintly.

" You can show him that *you* have the light on your soul ; that *you* know by experience the joy of a true believer ; that your religion is indeed your comfort ; that you have found that all her ways are ways of pleasantness, and that all her paths are peace."

The clergyman's words came to Io as a gentle reproof, and she accepted it in a child-like spirit. Its effect was deepened by a rude remark which had been made by Thud in the morning. "I have an idea," he had said, "that wives think it their duty to worry their husbands. You never thought of being so sickly and stupid before you were married."

CHAPTER XIII.

THE EXPEDITION.

WHEN Mr. Lawrence's short visit was ended, Io meditated over what she had heard with self-reproach and abasement.

"I have been adding to my Oscar's troubles," she said to herself, "instead of trying to lighten his burden. If he has indeed made a painful sacrifice to honour and duty, shall I, by my pride and sullen gloom, show him that as regards my happiness it has been made in vain? Shall I not gratefully accept the affection which he gives me, though it be not the all-absorbing, idolatrous love which my selfishness, my pride demands? May I not be risking all by requiring too much? That is my Oscar's step! with what joy I would once have sprung forth to meet him!" Io dried her eyes, and rose as Coldstream entered the veranda, an anxious, careworn look on his face.

"Io, my love, I have just been speaking with Pinfold about you," he said. "The doctor suggests that a change of air and scene might do you more good than medicine. What say you to a little camping out—an expedition to Tavoy ? "

" I should like it extremely," replied Io in her natural tone. She felt that it would be pleasant to escape from curious eyes, and wearisome inquiries after her health, to enjoy freedom in the wild woods, with Oscar for her companion. Her husband was pleased at the readiness and cheerfulness of her reply.

" You are not afraid of a little roughing it?" inquired Oscar tenderly, taking a seat beside his wife. " We should have to sleep in my little tent." He had taken Io's hand in his own, and was gently caressing it as he spoke.

" I should enjoy the life," was Io's reply ; " only, I was forgetting one thing : I could not leave my Maha behind, there is no lady in Moulmein to whom I could trust the poor child."

" You shall take Maha with you," said Oscar; " she shall share your tent at night, and wait on you by day."

" But where would you sleep, my Oscar ? "

" Under the trees—I've done so before; that is nothing to an old sportsman like me. A knapsack for a pillow, a rug for a bed—in this fine climate that is luxury enough for a man."

" For you, I daresay, but not for me," observed Thud, who had joined the Coldstreams in the veranda, and so had heard the conversation between them. " I have an idea that sleeping under trees is bad for the constitution."

"By all means remain under a roof," said Oscar, who was not anxious to have the company of Thucydides Thorn. "I shall ask Mr. Lawrence to let you live with him during our absence, and you will go on with your work at the wharf."

"With Mr. Lawrence!" said Thud dolefully; "I'd rather be sent to prison at once. Fancy being boxed up with a parson! I'd rather by far chum with Pogson."

"I will not consent to your chumming with Pogson. As long as your mother trusts you to my care, you must allow me to make your arrangements," said Coldstream, with that quiet decision which even Thud was learning to respect.

"Then I'll go to Tavoy," decided Thud. "I daresay that you can get another tent for my use."

"Not without expense and delay," replied Oscar. "I am anxious to start on Monday, so as, if possible, to reach Tavoy by the end of the week. Remember that all our luggage has to be carried on mules. A large cavalcade is not to be desired. I should like you to stay in Moulmein."

"And I should like to go to Tavoy," said the lad. "If I must sleep under a tree, I must. I'll have two rugs and a blanket. Camping out will give me fine opportunities of adding to my knowledge of natural history."

"Yes; you will have the opportunity of finding out

whether the mosquito has a proboscis not due to man's cultivation," said Io archly.

"How would you like to travel, my love?" inquired Oscar of his wife. "To ride your pony all the way would be far too fatiguing, and there is no proper carriage-road. What say you to a litter, or a howdah on an elephant's back?"

"I should like an elephant of all things," exclaimed Io, with so much of her old playfulness that Oscar's face relaxed into something like a smile.

"I should like it of all things too!" cried Thucydides Thorn.

"The howdahs used here are very small," observed Oscar; "there is room for but two persons in them."

"All right. You prefer walking, or riding a *tat* [country pony]; Io and I will sit in the howdah."

"You forget the young Karen," said Oscar. "She must sit with her lady."

"Oh, I say!" exclaimed Thud with more of the school-boy than of the philosopher in his manner and tone; "a dirty brown beggar on an elephant's back, and I on a wretched tat!"

"No one obliges you to go at all," observed Cold-stream.

But Thud was resolved to make one of the party, even if a tat were to be his only means of conveyance. Besides, he had thought of a less ignoble steed.

"I'll ride Io's pony, Lightfoot," said he.

" Io may choose sometimes to ride him herself," observed Oscar. " We shall take a lady's saddle with us."

" Besides that, dear Thud," said Io, " you might spoil Lightfoot's paces or harden his mouth ; you have only as yet ridden donkeys."

To be told that he did not know how to ride was an insult almost too great for Thud's philosophy to endure. He made a silent resolve that he *would* ride, and ride Lightfoot, but the presence of Coldstream prevented his making a reply. He only looked like an owl in the sulks.

Every one now was busy with preparations, and the work was good both for Oscar and Io. The latter felt her spirits rebound at the prospect of the change. Io resolved, if possible, to help Oscar to regain his lost cheerfulness, and not herself let her mind dwell on depressing thoughts.

" I will try to forget that such a being exists as Adelaide Mortimer," said Io to herself, as she dived into the depths of one of her large trunks, to bring out such things as would be most suited for the intended expedition. " I will try to forget that there was ever a woman who so came between me and my betrothed that to renounce her cost him a terrible illness, and has ever since darkened his life with gloom. Let a thick curtain be drawn over the past ; may grace be given me to make a better use of the present, and look forward with more hope and faith to the future ! "

Thud sauntered into the room where Io was standing surrounded by a heterogeneous collection of articles scattered on the floor, things hastily pulled out of the box to be replaced in it as soon as a selection should have been made. Thud had in him something of the forager as well as the sage: the owl does not think it below its dignity to pounce down on a mouse.

"Ah! that muslin—it will just suit me for a *pagri* [turban]; one must wear a *pagri* twisted round one's hat to keep off the heat of the sun even in what they call the cold weather."

"Take it, and welcome," said Io.

"And that piece of American waterproof cloth—that's just what I want," cried Thud.

"But I happen to want it too," said Io good-humouredly; "I brought it to wrap up the first parcel which I intend to send to dear mother in England."

"You can easily get more such cloth; you can wait, and I can't, if we're to start on Monday," said Thud. "You must make for me a big bag or case with a dozen pockets; I'll show you just what I want. I'll have a label sewn on each—one pocket for minerals, one for beetles, one for butterflies, one for feathers, one for eggs, one for my journal (for I must take no end of notes), and one for fishing-hooks and flies (for I must have ichthyological specimens too)."

"And is this big case to be hung round your neck?" asked Io.

"Not a bad idea, to have it handy. I could not get at it if it were packed amongst other luggage on a mule, and I shall be wanting it every minute."

Io was an indulgent sister. She gave the cloth and patient attention besides, and with the assistance of the *darzi* (tailor) the bag was made. Thud insisted on its being bound with red braid, also drawn from Io's stores, with strong strings of red ribbon to fasten it on securely. The lad looked at his "specimen case," as he called it, with pride : it was to be the nucleus of the museum which in his mind's eye he already beheld—a museum with portico and pillars, containing the valuable collection of Thucydides Thorn, with some eight or ten mysterious capitals after his name.

Thud appeared to be too busy even to go to church on the following Sunday. Notwithstanding Io's expostulations, she had to leave him to write labels and affix them on his specimen case.

CHAPTER XIV.

A DISCOVERY.

MONDAY came. The huge bulk of the elephant, with its howdah outside, darkened the veranda; servants were busy lading mules; there were boxes of provisions, the small tent, trunks, knapsacks, cooking vessels, and many other *et cætera* to be packed, the weight duly apportioned, and the ropes securely fastened. To start on a camping expedition in Siam is a very different thing indeed from going on a railway journey in England. Foresight is required, readiness of resource, and a large amount of patience; no necessary article must be forgotten, no possible contingency overlooked.

Io, who had completed her packing arrangements, sat in the drawing-room writing her letters for the English mail, to have them sent off before she should start. Every now and then she laid down her pen, that she might run to the veranda to see how the packing was progressing. The novelty and bustle of the scene were to the youthful Englishwoman somewhat amusing.

Io was just finishing her despatch when Oscar entered the room, with his little packet of letters in his hand.

"Is your letter to your mother ready?" said he. "We had better send off our budget to the post before we start."

Io folded up her large sheet in the then approved style (envelopes are a modern invention; paste wafers, now a thing of the past, were in common use then, when the more formal wax seal was not required). As lucifer matches were unknown, sealing was a more troublesome operation in those days than in the reign of our gracious Queen.

"Is all ready for our start?" asked Io, as she pressed the seal down on the wafer. "Is the luggage at last all packed on the mules, and Lightfoot saddled and bridled? I think that I shall set out on my pony."

"I am sorry to say that we cannot take Lightfoot at all," replied Oscar.

"Why? Nothing the matter, I hope?"

"Master Thud had his own reasons for staying away from church yesterday," answered Coldstream in a tone of displeasure. "The boy chose to ride Lightfoot, and let him down. Thud has no idea of riding."

"Oh, I hope that my poor pony is not much hurt!" cried Io.

, "Not permanently injured, I think," replied Oscar; "but he is lame, and must not be mounted till our return. I am annoyed at your disappointment, and have been rebuking Thud pretty sharply; but he is so encased in self-complacency that it is not easy to touch him. He told me that the fall was entirely the fault of the pony."

"I fear that poor Thud is a great trial to you, dear Oscar," observed Io.

"He would have been a greater trial to those at home. I do not regret that we brought him. I own that if we had any one with whom to leave him, Thud should not, after this last prank, accompany us to Tavoy. But I cannot burden poor Lawrence, and Pogson is out of the question—so are the Cottles."

"Dr. Pinny?" suggested Io.

Oscar Coldstream shook his head. "I would not say a word against your old friend," he observed; "but you yourself would hardly think the good doctor a desirable guardian for your young brother."

"No, perhaps not," said Io slowly, looking down as she spoke; and as she did so her eyes fell on the little packet of Oscar's letters which he had laid down on her writing-table whilst speaking of Thud. The address on the uppermost of those letters made Io start and flush to her temples. It was directed to *Mrs. Mortimer.*

"Who is she?" exclaimed Io, impatience and indignation forcing out the words against her will.

Oscar looked at his wife with surprise. "She is my more than friend," he replied. "You must often have heard of her from me."

"I never heard the name from your lips," exclaimed Io.

"What! not heard of my mother's old friend, my godmother—she who wrote to you so warmly after our engagement?"

"That was Mrs. Winter, the dear, sweet lady who nursed you through the small-pox when you were quite a little child."

"Mrs. Winter and Mrs. Mortimer are one. I must have forgotten to tell you of her second marriage, which took place when I was last in Moulmein. My friend married a cousin of her own who was going, in a state of hopeless consumption, to Malta. Mrs. Winter married him in order to be able to go with the dying sufferer and nurse him to the last."

"O Oscar, what a fool I have been!" exclaimed Io, bursting into tears; but the tears were those of relief, and shed on the bosom of her husband.

"And can it be," said Oscar, in a tone of gentle reproach, "that my Io for one moment thought me so base, so utterly worthless, as to be even in thought faithless to her to whom I had pledged my troth? Could you not trust me, Io?"

Io, very penitently, took her husband's hand and kissed it passionately. "Oh, forgive me, forgive me!" she sobbed; "we should never, never doubt one whom we love."

Oscar's reply was a heavy sigh, almost a groan.

Io looked up anxiously into his face. "O my beloved husband," she cried, "you have now found out the secret of my sadness; and now that you know all, my soul is relieved of its burden. Will you not also open your heart? will you not tell me why your life has lost its brightness? There should be no secret between husband and wife."

Oscar took both hands of his Io, and his eyes gazed into hers with an expression of mingled love and sorrow which she remembered to her dying day. "There should be no secret between us. Io, I would tell you everything were not your peace dearer to me than my own."

"Any knowledge is better than ignorance," exclaimed Io in an agitated tone.

"Did Eve find it so?" asked Oscar. "No, my beloved," he continued, still holding her hand in his own; "on this one subject you must not press me to speak. You cannot relieve me of my burden; you cannot even help me to bear it. Let this be the last time that you even allude to its existence. I ask only your silence and your prayers." Oscar pressed a tender kiss on Io's brow, took up his letters, and quitted the room.

CHAPTER XV.

MOUNT AND AWAY.

"Ha! ha! Master Thucydides Thorn, you are evidently a second Don Quixote, bent on adventures, or you would not start with a square yard of black sticking-plaster, bound 'with red rags to look like blood,' hanging round your neck! That is something like business. Ha! ha! ha!"

It was Dr. Pinfold who thus chatted and laughed. He had come to see Io start on her expedition, and was rejoiced to find his favourite looking already in much better health. Io's spirits had rebounded after their late depression, the cause of that depression having been suddenly removed. She looked bright and quite ready to enjoy herself as she gazed up laughingly at the elephant, wondering how she should ever reach the height of his back.

"Make the brute kneel to his lady, as in duty bound!" cried the doctor to the *kahaut* [driver], who was perched on the elephant's neck. The man shook his head, and jabbered something unintelligible to most of the party.

"He says that this elephant is not trained to kneel," said Oscar, coming up at the moment. "We have a short elephant-ladder which we will carry with us.—Io, my love, are you ready to mount?"

With the aid of her husband and the doctor Io very soon reached the howdah, and smiled down on those who had helped her to attain her lofty position.

"A little queen on her throne!" cried the doctor.

"Please help Maha too," said Io. But the active little Karen needed no help; she clambered up the steps like a cat.

"Now, knight of the sticking-plaster, let us see you on your tat," said Pinfold gaily.

"This is not sticking-plaster; do you not see the labels?" cried Thud. "This is what I am going to stow my specimens in—this is the nucleus of a museum."

"You'll have some rare treasures in it," said the merry doctor. "I hope you've left a pocket for bandages and salve, in case you come to grief in your specimen-hunting.—Coldstream, how do you travel?"

"On foot. I like the exercise," replied Oscar. "We shall proceed but slowly. I can easily keep up with the elephant."

"But hardly with the tat. Ha! ha! ha!—Mind, Thud, how you get up; the brute looks as if he were given to biting. No, no, don't venture behind him; he puts back his ears—he's certain to kick."

"Hold him, will you? and don't laugh!" cried Thucydides Thorn.   "I don't like the looks of the beast."

Awkwardly the heavy lad mounted, secretly regretting the accident to Lightfoot, which had prevented his having the chance of a better mount.   The Burmese tat might have tried the mettle of a better rider than Thud. First, Ma Ping—such was his name—determined not to stir from the spot.   In vain Thud tried to coax him to go on, then cautiously touched him up with the whip, Pinfold looking on and laughing.

"Give it him, Thud!" cried the doctor, bestowing on the tat a gratuitous whack with his own umbrella.

The unexpected blow from behind had instantaneous effect.   Ma Ping suddenly bolted off at a pace which almost unseated his rider.   Off came Thud's *pagri* and hat; but he clung desperately to the pommel with which the native saddle was happily furnished, without the aid of which the youth would certainly have come to the ground.

"'Away went Gilpin, who but he!'" exclaimed Pinfold in high glee; indeed, no one acquainted with Cowper's poem could have seen Thud at that moment without being reminded of the "citizen of credit and renown."   The tat's rapid motion had twisted round Thud's black case, and, hanging by its red strings, it streamed like a pennon behind him.

The tat was, however, brought up in its career by a cactus hedge; and Thud, panting and frightened but unhurt, awaited the coming up of the elephant and the rest of the party.

Thud made another attempt to arrange that Maha should change places with himself; the tat would suit a Karen, he declared, and he would prefer a howdah. But to this arrangement Oscar decidedly objected. He again gave his brother-in-law the alternative of remaining in Moulmein, but to this suggestion the lad would not listen. The specimen case was twisted round to its proper position, the hat and dusty *pagri* replaced, and Thud proceeded on his tat in rather a sulky condition.

Io enjoyed her ride; everything was to the youthful Englishwoman so strange and new. The party passed by paddy-fields, in which men and women were working together. The peasants stopped their labours to stare in wonder at a fair lady, who in return gazed down with curiosity upon them.

"O Oscar, look at that boy smoking a cigar three times the size of Dr. Pinny's, with another stuck in each ear! How strange everything looks to my English eyes! What wonderfully tall grass we are approaching! It would almost hide my elephant; the tat will be lost in it altogether. Graceful bamboos! with what dignity they raise aloft their feathery crowns; and surely that is a banyan, that tree of which I have read so often, that looks like a dark green roof resting on gnarled brown pillars, with big roots, like snakes, curling at their bases. This bird's-eye view of a new world is very amusing. What a flight of parrots—lovely green, screaming parrots! And see that bird with flashing blue wings—such an exquisite metallic tint! Certainly, if our English birds excel those of the East in song, these far excel ours in plumage."

With such cheerful chat Io Coldstream beguiled the way. Oscar encouraged his wife to talk, gathered for her wild flowers wherever he could see any remarkable for beauty, and bade Io employ Maha's deft fingers in making garlands for the howdah. He told stories of hunting adventures, and promised his wife specimens of birds to take home, as he had not forgotten to bring his gun.

"I think that my Oscar is getting back his spirits; the change is already doing him good," such was the hope which brightened everything to Io. She was almost sorry when the first stage of the journey came to an end, and the party halted to rest their animals, and themselves partake of a meal which they found ready cooked, as Coldstream had sent on servants in front to prepare it.

"Tired? Oh no, not in the least tired," cried Io, as her husband helped her down the elephant-ladder; "I am only hungry after my delightful ride."

"I'm famishing!" exclaimed Thud. "My ride has been anything but delightful. I'm as stiff as if I'd been beaten."

"There is still time for you to return," observed Oscar.

"I don't want to return; but I want to ride the elephant—he's a quiet, sensible sort of beast. Can't the beggar girl go on the tat?"

Again the proposition met with a decided negative from Oscar.

"It seems hardly worth while to pitch the tent now," observed Coldstream to Io; "we shall have to do so at night."

"But not now, oh, not now! with this delightful cluster of trees to spread over us their shade and shed their golden blossoms upon us," was the cheerful reply.

Thud ate ravenously, and then solaced himself for his fatigues and perils by sleeping on a soft, luxurious rug spread on the ground. Oscar, after his long walk, and with another before him, also stretched himself on the grass, but he did not sleep. He was listening to the voice of his Io, warbling to herself a sweet, happy lay. Io sang as the birds sing, pouring forth the rich notes as if they came spontaneously from a thankful, trustful heart :—

" The angry thunder-cloud
　　Pours its showers on the vine;
Safe in their downy shroud
　　Unhurt the clusters shine.
The raindrops trickle down the spray;
They cannot harm, they cannot stay.

" On ocean the sea-mew
　　Fearless braves the stormy weather,
Safe in the oily dew
　　On each soft and glist'ning feather.

Though o'er her dash the briny spray,
It cannot **harm**, it cannot stay.

" **In hours of grief** acute
   Thus peace religion brings,
Like the bloom upon the fruit,
   Or the oil upon the wings.
Though tears fall fast in sorrow's day,
They cannot harm, they cannot stay."

"Sing that again, my love," said Oscar.

"I did not know that you were listening; I thought that I had lulled you to sleep," said Io. "So you like my little song?"

"Your music is my solace," replied Oscar; "it tells me that you are happy, and to see you so is my greatest earthly desire."

"I have one song which you have not heard yet," observed Io. "I stole the air from the world; it is a pretty old English tune. You know that Luther said that the evil one should not have the best music."

"Sing it by all means," cried Oscar; and his wife cheerfully obeyed :—

" I'm waiting for the dawn **of day,**
   When joy shall **end earth's sin** and sadness,
When every shade shall pass away—
   The **world,** with all its guilt and madness.
Oh, how happy—Christ possessing—
Close, close to Him, the Fount of Blessing.
      His smile so bright,
      My joy, delight,
And every thought a thought of pleasure."

Thus Io sang song after song. To Oscar each one

seemed sweeter than the last. Was the loving minstrel not charming the dark spirit of sorrow away? It was not till the sun was sloping towards the west that, the burdens being replaced on the mules, Io and Maha mounted again to the howdah.

"This has been such a happy day!" observed Io to her husband, as again the little cavalcade moved on.

But the day was not to close without its adventure. Thud, tired of his troublesome tat, asked Oscar to mount the animal. "You may bring the brute into order; I don't mind walking a little. Perhaps I may find something to put into my specimen bag."

But Thud soon became weary of walking. A stubble field afforded no materials for his museum, and the path was thickly covered with dust. The tat, ridden by Oscar, looked quiet enough, and Thucydides Thorn expressed a wish to try him again.

Oscar dismounted, and held the tat's bridle to enable his companion to get up—a feat not very easily accomplished by Thud, who was awkward at mounting. But once in the saddle, the lad's self-confidence revived; he resolved to show his mastery over the tat.

"I understand him now," exclaimed the youth, shaking the rein and flourishing the whip. "I've a notion that an animal soon finds out what sort of man is on his back. My theory is—"

What Thud's theory was remains amongst things

unknown; for the tat made a sudden caper, first turning completely round, then darting with speed in the direction of Moulmein.

"Stop him! stop him!" cried Thud; and as the tat dashed past the loaded mules, one of the drivers tried to catch at the rein. The tat swerved, made a plunge, and Thud measured his short length on the dusty road!

"Oh, I trust that he is not hurt!" exclaimed Io, who was near the place where her brother had fallen, but who could not dismount without aid.

The reply came in a howl of mingled anger and pain from the prostrate rider. Oscar hastened to the spot where Thud, who had now raised himself to a sitting position, was roaring like a two-year-old child, and pressing his handkerchief to his mouth.

"Help me down, Oscar," cried the pitying Io. "I must see how much my poor boy is hurt."

"There is not much harm done, I think," observed Mr. Coldstream.—"Stand up and shake yourself, Thud. There are certainly no bones broken; the road was perfectly soft. Leave off crying, Thud; tears are unworthy of any one but a baby. There seems to be very little the matter."

"Little the matter!" howled Thud. "Would you have called the matter little if you had had your two front teeth knocked out?" and, removing his handkerchief, Thud showed a tear-stained face, with a mouth

whose beauty was by no means improved by an unsightly gap in the upper row of his teeth.

Thud carefully preserved the two teeth. Dr. Pinfold's prediction had come true : these rare treasures, at
least to their owner, were the first to be placed in the
specimen bag.

CHAPTER XVI.

THE LONE VILLAGE.

THUD could not be persuaded to mount Ma Ping again. Io pleaded to be allowed to walk, at least for a part of the stage; so she and Maha descended the elephant ladder, and for an hour Thud had the howdah all to himself. Coldstream then made the lazy lad descend, to walk the rest of the way, while his sister and her attendant resumed their places. Thud grumbled not a little, and thought the stage interminable. However, the halting-place for the night was reached at last: it was under a thick banyan tree, whose dense foliage would protect from the night dews those who had to sleep on the ground. The servants were busy pitching the small tent which Coldstream had brought for his wife.

"I can't sleep on the bare earth," said Thud doggedly; "it is so hard, and I should catch my death of cold."

"I am going to sleep on the ground," observed Oscar. "We have plenty of rugs and wraps. I have often made my bed beneath a tree."

" *You,* I daresay ; but I'm different. I've a theory that development of brain makes the bodily frame more delicate, and that philosophers need to sleep softer and fare better than other men."

" You were forewarned as to what you would have to meet," was Oscar's quiet reply.

" And then on the ground one is not safe from all sorts of reptiles—ants, caterpillars, centipedes, scorpions, snakes !" cried Thud, raising his voice to more emphatic pitch till he reached his climax of horrors.

" Specimens for your natural history collection," said Oscar.

" O Thud ! look at that glorious full moon rising over the plain ; feel the fresh, sweet air on your cheek. There is pleasure—luxury, in this camping out !" cried Io.

" For those who like it," growled Thud.

The night passed peaceably with the travellers ; even Thud had no cause to grumble. Coldstream was up with the first dawn of light. A magnificent imperial pigeon, and two green ones brought down by his gun, afforded the travellers a sumptuous breakfast, and put even Thud into comparative good-humour. Moreover, he put some of the feathers into his bag.

Then put howdah on elephant, saddle on tat, burdens on mules, and off and away !

The country soon changed its character as the travellers wended on their way. Instead of paddy-fields, bamboo clumps, and occasional groups of trees, the ground rose into hills, and progression became more difficult. The elephant came at last to places where it seemed to be impossible that so heavy an animal should make its way. At one spot there was an incline so steep that Io, though a girl of spirit, became a little nervous.

"I do not think that we *can* get down there," she said to her husband. "I should be frightened to see you attempt to ride down on the tat; the elephant would certainly come to grief."

"Can he manage it?" asked Coldstream of the *kahaut*, who was perched on the animal's neck.

"He manage it cleverly," was the reply.

And the creature did manage the descent cleverly. A sudden movement, which jerked Io and Maha backward in the howdah, and made them cling to its sides, gave notice that the huge beast which they rode had knelt on his hinder legs; then, putting the thick fore legs together, the elephant slid down the steep incline, and perfectly preserving his balance, landed safely at the bottom.

"I say, that's what I call clever!" cried Thud. "I should not like to have been on the back of the beast!"

"My brave wifie!" exclaimed Oscar; "you did not look in the least afraid."

"But I felt so—rather; and I held on very fast," was the candid reply.

The descent was also cleverly managed by the active little tat and the sure-footed mules. Only Thud concluded his performance of the feat by a roll in the dust.

After proceeding for another hour the travellers came in sight of a village nestling under the shelter of a palm-crowned height.

"What a picturesque little place, with its bamboo huts and thatched roofs!" exclaimed Io. "I wish, Oscar, that you had brought your sketch-book as well as your gun."

"The village would make a good subject for a picture, and is pleasing at a distance," said Oscar. "But peaceful and fair as it looks, how much of vice, misery, superstition, and idolatry are likely to be found in its dwellings!"

"I do not like to think that," said Io. "See the cattle grazing about, and the goats with their kids; look at the buffaloes enjoying themselves in the big pond, with only their snouts and horns above the surface of the water."

"Where there are cows I have an idea that there must be milk," observed Thud. "I'm as thirsty as a frog, and as tired as a hack on Holborn Hill."

"Oh! a drink of milk would be a luxury," cried Io.

"I will try to procure some at once," said her husband.

"Might we not go to the village ourselves?" suggested Io; "it would be something so novel, so amusing."

Io's slightest wish was a law to Oscar. The little ladder was at hand, and he helped his wife to descend from her lofty perch. Maha, as before, needed no assistance.

"She's a kind of monkey," observed Thud with contempt.

The party proceeded towards the village, Io leaning upon the arm of her husband. By the side of the path sat a very old man, wrinkled and bent. He lifted up his head at the sound of strangers' feet, and the Coldstreams then perceived that he was quite blind.

"Blind, poor, and so old!" exclaimed Io. "Oscar dear, have you a coin about you?"

The coin was produced and silently dropped by Io into the old man's hand.

"The Lord reward you!" ejaculated the old native in the Karen tongue.

The Coldstreams were surprised at the expression used.

"You have had a hard life, father," said Io gently.

"There is a better life to come," was the Karen's reply. "I shall soon be with my Saviour."

"Who is your Saviour?" asked Io.

"The Lord Jesus Christ," answered the blind Karen, reverently bowing his hoary head.

"From whom have you heard of Him?" asked Oscar with interest.

"From our brother, Ko Thah Byu," was the slowly-uttered reply.

A little farther on, a small girl, very scantily dressed, was happily engaged in sucking a bit of sugar-cane.

She took it out of her mouth, and looked up in innocent wonder as the Europeans approached her.

"She will be our little guide," observed Oscar.—"My child," he said to the girl, "will you take us to the house of your mother?"

The girl understood him, but shook her black locks. Oscar repeated his question.

"Mother up there—with the Lord," said the child, pointing to the blue, cloudless sky.

"Who told you that your mother had gone to the Lord?" asked Io.

The same reply came from the child as had been uttered by the old man, "Brother Ko Thah Byu."

"This is very striking—very, very interesting," said Io. "Hark! is not that the sound of a gong? There are boys gathering under yon tree."

"I daresay to worship some hideous idol," suggested Thud. "It is not safe to disturb savages at their horrible rites." Thud had not understood a word of the Karen language spoken, and his ideas of savages were principally taken from "Robinson Crusoe."

"There is no idolatry here," observed Io. "The boys, in orderly fashion, are sitting down in a circle. This looks for all the world like a little school. The gong only summoned the pupils."

"We will go nearer and inquire," said Oscar.

Yes, it was a school in that secluded village in Siam. The master was a simple Karen peasant, and his lesson-book a portion of the Bible. The Coldstreams felt as if they had unexpectedly lighted on a jewel.

"Who started this school?" inquired Oscar of the Karen teacher, who rose from his squatting position in surprise, whilst all his young, half-naked pupils forgot their lessons to gaze open-mouthed on the apparition of a white lady wearing a hat and veil.

"Who started this school?" repeated Oscar.

"Brother Ko Thah Byu," was the reply.

"He must be a very remarkable man," observed Oscar to his wife. "I am very sorry that I did not meet him when he was actually passing through Moulmein."

"I would give anything to see this Karen apostle," said Io.

The visitors were hospitably treated in the Karen village : not only milk, but *kur* (coarse brown sugar) and rice were placed before them, and when Oscar offered payment it was refused. Further inquiries regarding Ko Thah Byu elicited the information that this evangelist had successfully preached the gospel in many places, both in Burmah and Siam, but that it had been most welcomed by those of his own Karen race, who were scattered in both countries, often greatly oppressed, except where protected by the power of the English, to whom the Karen Christians seemed greatly attached.*

* It is a remarkable fact that when the English, many years after the date of my story, took possession of Upper Burmah, they trusted Karens with weapons, and found them do good work as gallant police in bringing that troublesome district into order.

" Our white brothers, who came by water as our great father foretold, spread a big shield over the poor Karens," said the village teacher; "our white brothers are welcome."

The Coldstreams and Thud remained some time in the hospitable village of Mouang. Maha was delighted to find herself amongst her own people, and laughed and chatted gaily with the women. The party quitted Mouang with regret, and Io said that the hour spent with the Christian Karens had been amongst the happiest of her life.

CHAPTER XVII.

IN THE FOREST.

AGAIN the little cavalcade moved forward, and again Oscar heard a sweet voice warbling from the height of the howdah. Well he knew that the song was meant for his ear.

"Thank Heaven! Io is happy," thought he; "happy in pure memories of the past, in the innocent joys of the present, and in the unclouded hope of the glory to come. What a strange fate it was that linked this bright, joyous being's life to mine! Will Io miss me in the mansions of light? Amidst her thoughts of gladness will there be one of tender regret for one who loved her as no other man ever loved?"

It was not long before Oscar's attention had to be given to new difficulties on the road. The path, for it was not a highway, led through a dense forest, where thick branches interlaced above formed an unexpected barrier which no elephant carrying a howdah could possibly pass.

"Oscar, what is to be done?" exclaimed Io, as the huge animal which she rode came to a sudden halt.

"This is very annoying," said Oscar. "I was assured that the road the whole way to Tavoy might be traversed on an elephant's back. I will send men to the right and left to ascertain if indeed there be no practicable path through the wood."

The search was made in vain. There was evidently no way to proceed but through the tangled forest. Oscar, who had joined in the search, came back to his wife.

"It is evidently impossible to go on," said he. "No howdah could pass under these trees."

"Then what is to be done?" repeated Io. "I can hardly attempt to walk the whole way to Tavoy," she added, in as cheerful a tone as she could command; "and if I tried the tat without a lady's saddle, I fear that I should come to grief, like Thud."

Oscar reflected for a moment. "We might try what I first proposed—a litter."

"What! make an improvised one of branches?" cried Io gaily. "But where are the bearers to carry me?"

"We had better return to our new friends at Mouang," observed Oscar; "they may supply us with some rude substitute for litters, and men to carry them also."

"But if you go back to the village it makes the distance greater," growled Thud. "I am already walked off my legs; my boots have holes, and my feet are blistered."

"Get up on the elephant, Thud," said Io. "Maha and

I will walk back to Mouang; I shall really enjoy the change."

The lofty seat in the howdah just suited the taste of Thucydides Thorn, who liked to look down on the rest of the world, and feel himself in the high position to which he was always aspiring. Oscar did not wish the laden mules to return—they could make their way through the wood; and his servants had to prepare food and pitch the tent at the end of the next long stage.

Io had a delightful walk by the side of Oscar, and found the distance to the village only too short.

The Karens were surprised at the travellers making so speedy a return, though the shrewder amongst them had guessed that the elephant would never get through the forest. The villagers welcomed the party very kindly. Coldstream soon made the Karens understand what he required. Litters there were none at Mouang, but rude substitutes could be made out of *charpais* (small bedsteads), ropes, and the bamboos which were abundant. Nothing was required but dexterity and a moderate space of time. The Karens cheerily lent their aid; Oscar not only gave directions, but worked vigorously with his own hands; Io and Maha helped to tie ropes and spread rugs over the improvised litters. Thud, without descending from the howdah, watched all at their work with his thumbs in his pockets. He felt himself to be a presiding genius.

Though the best possible speed had been made, some

hours passed before the litters were completed, and the Karens who were to carry them were ready to start.

" What is to be done with the elephant ? " asked Thud.

" The elephant must return to Moulmein," was Coldstream's reply ; " he cannot carry his howdah through land clothed with thick forest trees."

" Then I'll return with him," cried Thud. " I've had enough and too much of gipsy life, going on tramp up hill and down hill, tearing one's clothes, scratching one's skin, spoiling one's boots, and hurting one's feet. I'll go back to more civilized life."

It cannot be said that either Oscar or Io regretted their brother's wish to turn back. The former, however, exacted a promise from the lad that he would put up at the chaplain's house till his sister's return, and go on with work at the office. So the party separated, the elephant going one way and the litters the other, the Karens willingly carrying the latter, pleased with the liberal pay which the English gentleman offered.

" Good-bye, Thud," cried out Io, looking up and waving her hand to her brother. " I hope that you will have filled every pocket in your bag before our return."

Thucydides grinned, displaying the unsightly gap in his row of front teeth, and secretly resolving to show his sister something worth seeing. He had a theory that he could produce black blossoms on her fine creepers by watering them with ink ! Thud had also an idea that Lightfoot might be cured of his lameness by steady application of mustard plasters.

"Let's make the best haste that we can," said Io, as she seated herself on her litter. "The delay has made me more than ready for dinner. Thud has carried off our sandwich-box and all the biscuits, and the sun is getting low."

"We must indeed make the best speed we can," said Coldstream. "It is not desirable to go through the forest at night, for the thick foliage cannot be penetrated by the rays of the moon. Had I known how long we should be delayed at Mouang, I would have ordered my men to stop and pitch our tent at this side of the wood."

"I wish that we had torches," suggested Io.

"I took the precaution of securing two, and oil to feed them, when we were at Mouang," said Oscar.

The party reached the edge of the forest just as the sun's round red globe touched the horizon.

"Our people have evidently gone on," observed Oscar; "we can see the track of feet and hoofs on the path before us."

"Then we had better follow, and quickly too," cried Io, "for we can have neither food nor tent till we catch up with the mules."

Entering the sombre forest was almost like plunging into sudden night, so dense was the leafy shade. Coldstream ordered the peasants to light the torches, that there might be no risk of losing the track of the party in front. Io admired the picturesque effect of the red light on huge trunks, gnarled roots, and overhanging boughs, and suppressed, as far as she could, all signs of fatigue and hunger. She could not help thinking of the possibility of leopards, even tigers, haunting those dark, desolate woods. Her ear was quick to detect the slightest sound which imagination might convert into a distant growl, and her glance anxiously scanned the thick undergrowth of bushes to detect the glare of the eye of any wild beast. Oscar had left his gun on one of the mules : except that a few of the Karens had sticks, the party were utterly unarmed and defenceless in case of attack.

Io kept her fears to herself, and whenever she addressed her husband, did so in as cheerful a tone as she could command ; but she was exceedingly weary. Oscar walked on silently, being anxious on account of his wife, except when he broke the stillness of the woods by a shout, in hopes that the muleteers might not be far ahead, but able to hear and reply. At last the travellers came to an open space in the forest, which had been formerly cleared for the erection of an idol temple, of which a few ruins still remained. The moon, now from almost vertical height, threw her silvery light on these ruins and the dark encircling wood around. From this open space the road divided ; two ways appeared before the travellers, one bearing towards the right, one towards the left. The party came to a halt.

"It is evident which path the muleteers have taken," observed Oscar, as both moonlight and torchlight showed the marks of hoofs and naked feet on the road which bore to the left.

"Wrong—go wrong; way to Tavoy lie that way!" cried the foremost Karen, who bore one of the torches, pointing towards the right.

"Are you certain of that?" asked Oscar.

Almost with one voice the Karens replied, "Mules gone wrong way—drivers know nothing—never get to Tavoy."

Oscar felt extremely annoyed and perplexed. His wife, faint with fasting, might have to spend the whole night in the wood. Io was keeping up bravely, but her husband knew that she suffered. He was undecided as to what course to pursue: if he took the right path, he gave up hope of overtaking the mules which carried the tent and provisions; if he took the left, he and his party might be lost in the dark depths of the forest. Oscar thought of returning to Mouang; but he had already gone so far that he was unwilling to retrace his steps.

"Which course shall we take?" said Coldstream to his wife, after explaining to her the difficulty of coming to a decision.

"Let us ask God to guide us, dearest," was the reply of Io, a reply given with a smile, though she was struggling to keep down tears.

CHAPTER XVIII.

RESCUED.

THE question was decided in a startling manner. First, there was the sound of crashing of boughs, as if wild beasts were forcing their way through the thicket; then a burst of yells, which certainly came from human throats. The Karens started with alarm, put down the litters, and cried out, " Shans," which Coldstream knew to be the name of a tribe living farther towards the north. The next minute the clearing in the wood was filled with a wild band of half-clothed Siamese, shouting and flourishing rude weapons which flashed in the moonlight. Coldstream had no time to make even an attempt at resistance. The Shans knew that the Englishman was the one of the party most likely to show fight, so they made a determined rush from all sides on the unarmed man. A heavy blow brought Oscar to the earth, and as he struggled to regain his feet a dozen dark hands seized him, and with ropes wrenched from Maha's small litter Coldstream was tightly bound to a tree with his arms fastened behind him The whole affair passed so rapidly that the bewildered, terrified Io had scarcely time to understand what had happened before she saw her husband a helpless prisoner, and herself in the hands of a wild, lawless band! Io's alarm was great, but even her terror was as nothing compared to the agony of mind endured by her husband, who forgot his own danger in witnessing hers. Oscar could not even gasp forth a prayer; the fearful thought which had come to him before, that he was doomed to suffer through the wife whom he passionately loved, came on him again with agony so intense that a dagger plunged into his side would have inflicted less pain. Could Oscar's thoughts have been clothed in words they would have been, "I refused to pluck out the right eye; and now *both* eyes will be torn from me, and nothing remain to a wretch but the blackness of darkness for ever."

It was a terrible moment, but scarcely more than a moment, for suddenly, as if he had dropped from the skies, another form appeared on the scene. The Shans who had seized the shrieking Maha relaxed their grasp and fell back; they evidently recognized the new-comer, and re-echoed the exclamation which burst from the lips of every one of the Karens, "Ko Thah Byu!"

The Karen evangelist strode fearlessly into the very midst of the throng, and sternly wrenched away a dark hand that was grasping the shoulder of Io. The Shans fell back as if awed by the presence of one whom they knew to be a messenger of God.

Ko Thah Byu was not a man of majestic presence, nor did his appearance denote remarkable personal strength. He was past the meridian of life, and his dark hair and eyebrows were here and there streaked with white; but the eyes that flashed under those grizzled brows, and his firm, resolute mouth, marked the Karen as one born to exercise sway over his fellow-men. It has been written of the Karen apostle, when he had been seen preaching to a large congregation of Burmese, that "their attention seemed to be riveted on his flashing eyes, less apparently from love than from an indescribable power that may best be compared to the fascinating influence of the serpent over an unconscious brood of chickens."

Like a master startling his slaves in the commission of an act of disobedience, Ko Thah Byu's silent look conveyed stern reproof to the robbers. One glance, one gesture of his hand, and a Shan at once gave up to the Karen a gleaming knife. Ko Thah Byu walked up to the tree to which Oscar was tied and cut his bonds. Not a single word had been spoken by the singular Karen, but when he opened his lips there came forth a burst of indignant eloquence, unintelligible to his English hearers, who knew not the dialect of the Shans, but which had evidently a thrilling effect on the untutored listeners around. The Shans shrank back, as if ashamed, while a murmur of assent and applause burst from the Karens.

Then the stern manner of Ko Thah Byu changed, and

with simple native courtesy he approached Mr. Cold-stream, whom he addressed in the Karen language.

"Let not our white brother and sister fear aught," he said; "no one will lay a finger upon them."

At a gesture from Ko Thah Byu the Karens began trying to replace the ropes that had been wrenched from Maha's litter.

"No use—they have been cut. I will walk; my brothers are around me," said Maha.

Only Karens were left, for the Shans were retiring into the jungle from which they had so unexpectedly emerged.

"Will the sahib and mem return to Mouang?" said Ko Thah Byu. "It is not well to pass through the forest at night."

Oscar assented by a silent inclination of the head. At first he could not utter a word, the revulsion from utter despair was so great. Io made up for her husband's silence by giving fervent thanks to her deliverer in broken Karen, as she resumed her seat on her litter.

"It was all God's doing, mem sahib," said Ko Thah Byu in gentle tones, which curiously contrasted with his loud, impassioned address to the Shans. "Ko Thah Byu was on his way to Mouang, hoping to reach it before night should make the forest path dark. Ko Thah Byu sat by yon ruin, and read his book, and fell asleep, like the man in the pilgrim-story of whom the *padri* [clergyman] tells. Ko Thah Byu rose, and forgot his book, and went on his way, and trod many steps towards Mouang ere his loss was known. Karen servant of Christ had to go back; but he found the book, and now the reason why he lost it is clear as the moon in the sky. Karen at Mouang would not know of the white mem's trouble; Karen in the wood could give help. All was right—all is ever right that our Father God does for His children."

"All was indeed ordered in mercy," observed Io to her husband as he walked beside her litter, which was borne on again by the Karens. "My Oscar, at the worst, the very worst, I thought that the Lord would come to our help. I prayed very hard in my terror, and I am sure that you prayed too."

"No, I did not pray," was the gloomy reply, which astonished and distressed the young wife.

"O Oscar! I felt as if the Lord's loving hand were holding me up," she exclaimed.

"You saw the hand stretched forth to save; I saw the hand upraised to strike."

Oscar had no sooner uttered the unguarded words than he wished them unsaid. The party were passing under the deep shadow of the dark trees; the torches were some way in front. Oscar could not see on his wife's face the effect of the sentence which had escaped from him in a moment of anguish; still less could he know its effect on her mind, for Io uttered not another

word until Mouang was reached. The exclamation of
Oscar had been to her like a fearful revelation—a sudden
gleam on a dark subject, but such a gleam as a flash of
forked lightning might give.

"Oscar not pray—at such a moment of peril not be
able to pray!" so ran Io's troubled current of thought.
"He—the noble, the good, the pious—he could only see
our loving Father's hand upraised to strike! What
fearful mystery lies beneath this? We have long seen
my husband's sadness, and made guesses—oh, what
wrong guesses!—as to its cause. What could so shut out
a Christian from communion with God but *sin?* My
beloved one's life is as pure as mortal's can be; there
can be nothing in the present to weigh so heavily on his
conscience as to crush out the spirit of prayer. Can it
be possible that there has been something in the past
which to one so sensitive to the least touch of evil, one
who so abhors the smallest error, may appear to be a
very serious sin? Oh that Oscar would confide all to
his wife, to one who would not love him less whatever
he might have done!"

Then Io's thoughts fell naturally into the channel of
prayer. She had very often before pleaded for her
husband—she had wrestled in intercession at the time of
his illness, and again and again after her marriage—but
never with more intense, agonized earnestness than she
did now, with her litter for an oratory, and the black,
sombre night as a curtain around her. Her head bowed

on her clasped hands, and the tears wetting her pale cheeks, Io prayed in the gloomy forest. Then suddenly the litter emerged into moonlight, and the calm holy brightness around seemed like an earnest of answer to prayer.

"We are going for the third time to Mouang," thought Io as she leant back in her litter and closed her eyes, Oscar thought in sleep. "It seems as if some invisible cord drew us to a spot of which yesterday we knew not even the name. May it be that some strange blessing awaits us there. May it be that the guiding Hand which is leading us on in this land of strangers is taking us to a place where my Oscar's darkness will pass away, and where he will see and know that goodness and mercy have followed, and will follow him still, all the days of his life."

CHAPTER XIX.

THE PREACHER.

So entirely was Io absorbed in prayer that she did not notice when Mouang was reached.

"What are your wishes, my love?" asked Oscar, as he helped his wife out of the litter. "Shall we to-morrow proceed again towards Tavoy, or return to Moulmein?" Coldstream had to repeat the question before Io could even understand it; she was like one awakened from sleep.

"I do not wish to go on," Io then replied in a faint voice. "Let us rest for a while in the village if you will, and then go back to our home."

Io's extreme quietness disturbed Oscar; it was not in her nature to be so passive. There was no talking over the night's adventures, no remarks about the Karen deliverer. If she spoke, it was like one who speaks in a dream.

"It is the effect of past terror," said Oscar to himself; but he was mistaken in the supposition. Io had almost for the time forgotten the danger through which she had passed, her mind was so filled with the question, " What can it be that separates my beloved from his God ? "

The Karen villagers were asleep in their huts when, at the dead of night, the travellers approached Mouang ; but the voice of Ko Thah Byu soon roused them from their slumbers. Everything that could be done for the comfort of the white strangers was done with all possible haste. The family who occupied the cleanest bamboo hut hospitably gave it up to the lady. It was not the hour for milking cows or goats, fruit was scarce, bread and green vegetables not to be had ; but a fire was lighted, rice hastily boiled, and dried river-fish, with the dainties of red chillies and garlic, with leaves for plates, supplied the Coldstreams and Maha with a midnight meal. Io could eat little—her appetite was gone ; but she was thankful to lie down and rest, and try to forget her troubles in sleep.

Io was awakened in the morning by the beating of a small gong suspended from the branch of a tree. She started to a sitting posture, a little alarmed by the sound.

" It is only the call for the villagers to assemble for morning prayer," said Oscar, entering the hut with a large earthen vessel of fresh milk in his hand. " Would you like to be present, my love ? "

Io assented ; and Oscar, who had been up for some time, left her to make her morning preparations, and offer up her early devotions. During the course of

the night, the lost mules with their drivers had made
their appearance at Mouang, Ko Thah Byu having sent
a Karen guide after them to show them the way.

Before Io rejoined her husband, the early meeting for
prayer was half over. It was held in the open air:
peasants, men and women, some of the latter with babes
in their arms and little children beside them, listened to
the parable of the rich man and Lazarus, which Ko Thah
Byu, standing on a slight eminence, read and expounded.
The Scriptures which missionaries had caused to be
translated and printed in the tongue of the Karens, was
a treasure gladly welcomed and still dearly prized by
this people.

A fragment of one of Ko Thah Byu's addresses having
been preserved in his memoir, is inserted here, as a
specimen of the untutored eloquence of this remarkable
man. The evangelist, in his own impressive and
vehement way, denounced that love of the world and its
pleasures which is found even in the secluded villages
from which one might deem such temptations excluded.

"A worldly man is never satisfied with what he
possesses. Let me have more houses, more lands, more
buffaloes, more slaves, more clothes, more children and
grandchildren, more gold and silver, more paddy and
rice, more boats and vessels; let me be rich: this is his
language. He thinks of nothing so much as of amassing
worldly goods; of God and religion he is quite un-
mindful. But watch that man. On a sudden his

breath departs; he finds himself deprived of all he possessed and valued so much. He looks around, and sees none of his former possessions. Astonished, he exclaims, 'Where are my slaves? where are my buffaloes? I cannot find one of them! Where are my houses and my chests of money? What has become of all my rice and paddy that I laid up in store? Where are the fine clothes which cost me so much? I can find none of them. Who has taken them? And where are my wives and children? Ah, they are all missing; I can find none of them. I am lonely and poor indeed—I have nothing!' But what is this?" The impassioned preacher here entered upon a description of the sufferings of the sinner that is lost; after which he represented the rich man as taking up this lamentation: "Oh, what a fool I have been! I neglected God, the only Saviour, and sought only worldly goods while on earth, and now I am undone."

"All in this world is misery," pursued the preacher: "sickness and pain, fear and anxiety, old age and death, abound on every hand. But hearken; God speaks from on high: 'Children, why take ye delight and seek happiness in that low village of mortality, that thicket of briers and thorns? Look up to Me; I will deliver you and give you rest, where you shall be for ever blessed and happy.'"

CHAPTER XX.

DARK MEMORIES.

THE mules having returned and had some hours' rest, there was nothing now which need delay the travellers' departure from the village; but Oscar wished to see a little more of the Karen apostle before starting for Moulmein. After partaking of breakfast with his wife, Mr. Coldstream quitted the hut, and went in search of Ko Thah Byu. On inquiring where he could be found, one of the peasants directed Coldstream to a small clump of bushes with the remark, " Ko Thah Byu read—pray —alone."

Though hesitating a little as to whether he should intrude on the solitude of the Karen preacher, Oscar yet overcame his scruples, as another opportunity for conversation with his preserver might not occur. Coldstream found Ko Thah Byu seated on a large mossy stone, with his Bible on his knee; he was in the act of closing the holy book when the Englishman appeared, and the Karen rose to meet him.

"I have not yet thanked you, as I now do from my

heart," said Mr. Coldstream, "for my own preservation, and, far more, for that of my wife. Only show me how I can prove my gratitude. Is there anything that I can offer—"

An expressive movement of the native's brown hand, and a contraction of his brow, made Mr. Coldstream pause. Oscar felt that it would be as impossible to press gold on this moneyless Karen as upon a European noble. It was scarcely necessary for Ko Thah Byu to express his thoughts in words, though he did so with a native dignity which gave them force. "Ko Thah Byu wants nothing from his white brother. Ko Thah Byu did only his duty. Keep money for those who need."

"I should like to have a little conversation with you, my friend," said Mr. Coldstream, seating himself on the trunk of a felled tree which happened to be near, and motioning to the Karen to resume his former seat. "I should like to know something of your former history; I desire to hear what it was that first led to God one whom I regard as one of the noblest of men."

"*The noblest of men!*" repeated Ko Thah Byu with an emphasis of scorn that had in it something almost savage. "The sahib knows not of whom he speaks. *The noblest of men!*" again repeated the Karen. "A few summers past, if the demons of hell had been asked, 'Who is blacker than we? who should have a deeper place in the pit?' the demons would have clapped their hands and yelled out, 'Ko Thah Byu!'" Then the fierce expression on the Karen's stern features strangely softened, and his voice became soft as a woman's as he went on, "And now if the angels in heaven be asked, 'Who should praise most of all? who should wet Christ's feet with most tears, and kiss them with most exceeding great love?' the angels would lift up their hands and cry, 'Ko Thah Byu! Ko Thah Byu! for he has been most forgiven!'"

"Can this be so?" exclaimed Oscar Coldstream: "were you, before your conversion, so much worse than other men?"

"In childhood Ko Thah Byu was wicked—ungovernable," was the reply. "The sapling was crooked, bent, and black; what could the tree become? Even now Ko Thah Byu has in his heart a fierce wild beast that is chained, but which too often breaks his chain, and then men wonder that the Karen Christian should be so unlike his Master."*

Coldstream looked at the Oriental's rugged features and flashing eyes, and could imagine how formidable his bursts of passion might be if not tamed down and subdued by grace.

"Ko Thah Byu was a slave once," pursued the Karen, "knowing nothing—very dark—man's slave and a slave of Satan. Padri Judson set slave free from man's bonds, but the worse bonds held him tightly still. Ko Thah Byu then learned something of the good, but he fol-

* Ko Thah Byu's account of himself is strictly authentic.

lowed the bad. Got debt; Christian brother **Ko Shway Bay** paid debt—took **Ko Thah Byu** as servant. But servant bad, very bad; master could not keep such servant—sent him away. All men say Ko Thah Byu no Christian, **Ko Thah Byu** got very black heart. But Good Shepherd see that leopard could be turned into sheep; Christ could change wild beast's spots, Christ could put love in black dead heart. The Lord caught Ko Thah Byu when sinner just dropping into hell—over edge, falling down, down, down—Christ caught hold, and saved, and pulled sinner up, and washed, and set upon Rock!" Tears gushed from the Karen's dark eyes as he told of redeeming love.

"You had fierce temper and evil habits," observed Coldstream, who was listening with intense interest to the tale of the convert; "but you had perhaps never committed any great crime."

"Many," was the Karen's reply, uttered with startling vehemence. "God commands, *No steal;* Ko Thah Byu great robber. God commands, *Do no murder;* Ko Thah Byu wound, stab, kill!"

"Did you kill a man?" exclaimed Oscar, starting to his feet from emotion too strong to be repressed.

"Kill many men, more than these fingers thrice told," was the reply of **Ko Thah Byu,** as he stretched out his dark muscular hands.

"And you yet found grace—a murderer found grace!" cried Oscar.

"Sahib, Christ's blood wash even murderer white," was the earnest reply; "washed David, who sinned the murderer's sin. David's song is Ko Thah Byu's song, the history of Ko Thah Byu's life;" and with a fervour that appropriated every word as if it were a spontaneous burst from his own heart, the Karen repeated the first part of the thirty-second psalm, which fell on Oscar with all the force of a new revelation :—*Blessed is he whose transgression is forgiven, whose sin is covered. Blessed is the man unto whom the Lord imputeth not iniquity, and in whose spirit there is no guile. While I kept silence, my bones waxed old through my roaring all the day long. For day and night Thy hand was heavy upon me: my moisture is turned into the drought of summer.* The Karen's voice dropped, his head drooped; he seemed again to feel the crushing pressure, the wasting thirst of the soul, and was too much occupied with his own memories to notice the effect of his words on his hearer. Then raising his head again, and looking upwards with such a glance as seemed to tell of heaven itself opening before him, Ko Thah Byu went on with the psalm :—*I acknowledged my sin unto Thee, and mine iniquity have I not hid. I said, I will confess my transgressions unto the Lord; and Thou forgavest the iniquity of my sin.*

For the first time since, when a boy, he had stood by a mother's grave, Oscar Coldstream was sobbing!

He started on hearing a step, and turned a few paces

aside, that no one might see his agitation. A Karen had come to call Ko Thah Byu to the hut of a peasant taken suddenly ill. The evangelist hastened to the place, and Oscar was left alone with his thoughts. With his back turned towards the abodes of men, the Englishman strode up and down, and the exclamation burst from his lips, " But for Io, I would tell all, and find peace."

CHAPTER XXI.

CONFESSION.

"WHAT would Oscar do but for Io? is it Io who keeps him from peace?" A white trembling hand was on Coldstream's arm, and he turned to meet the wistful, pleading gaze of his wife, whose light footstep he had not heard when she came to seek him. Her husband could not reply.

"O Oscar—my life! there is some terrible secret which you would keep even from me. You have done something—something wrong. This is like a thorn in your conscience; you cannot find peace until it is taken away." Io unconsciously pressed very tightly the arm which she grasped.

"I cannot take the thorn out of my own breast to plant it in yours," said her husband.

"I would welcome it, if my sorrow could give you peace," exclaimed Io. "Mine own, my beloved, tell me all; let me judge—let your Io judge whether there is anything too painful for her to suffer, if she can only help to remove from her Oscar this secret, terrible pain.

It is my desire—my entreaty—my *right*—at least to judge for myself."

"Judge then, for you shall know all. I will hide nothing, even if confession should rob me of my most precious possession—your affection," said Oscar gloomily, motioning to Io to sit down on the large trunk, and then taking his place at her side. Io would have rested her head on her husband's breast, but he made a movement to prevent her so doing. "Not now, not now," murmured Oscar; "wait till you have heard all."

Io waited for several minutes till Oscar should break the silence which followed. She felt somewhat as a wretch condemned to be blown from a cannon might feel while awaiting the fatal explosion. When Oscar spoke at last it was with rapid utterance, as if to shorten suspense and pain.

"You remember our happiness at the time of our engagement—happiness almost perfect, till one day I showed petulance, and cost you the first tears which I ever saw you shed."

"Yes," replied Io sadly: "you were annoyed when Walter climbed higher than yourself to bring a flower from a very steep place, and I was foolish enough to put the flower in my hair. I was a silly, vain child," she added humbly. "It was new to me to be loved as you loved me; I am afraid that I liked to tease, and show my power by playing with your feelings."

" A woman who does so plays with edge-tools," muttered Oscar.

" But all was set right at once," cried Io. " I convinced you that I had never loved any man but yourself; that I merely amused myself with poor Walter because he was my cousin, brought up in the same nursery, and I liked his fun and his practical jokes. Surely I quite convinced you, Oscar ? "

" You did convince me, Io. I saw that I had been a jealous, unreasonable fool. You and I were happy once more."

" And it was never possible that my unfortunate cousin could give you a moment's uneasiness again," said Io. " He died about the time of your return. Walter had made a foolish bet that he would climb an inaccessible cliff; he failed—fell—and, alas ! perished."

" Walter did not fail, nor fall—till he was thrown down by these accursed hands," said Oscar abruptly. He dared not look at his wife as he spoke; he could not have met her look of horror.

" Now you know why I could not lead the devotions of others, why I dared not approach the Holy Table. Could I—wretch that I am—offer up petitions with guilty lips, take the emblems of redeeming love into a murderer's blood-stained hand ? No, I could not have so played the hypocrite, or I might have been struck dead on the spot."

" I cannot believe this frightful tale," gasped Io;

"you have been dreaming it in some fit of delirium. Why should you injure my poor cousin, from whom you parted in friendship, and whom you had not even seen for two years ?"

"You know the worst; now hear what may possibly extenuate a little my madness—my guilt." Oscar spoke in a calmer tone, for he already felt something of relief from frank confession. "When I started from Moulmein to return and claim you as my bride, I was the happiest mortal on earth. Paradise seemed to open before me. The first check to my joy came at Malta, where I found no letter from Io."

"The one which Thud detained told you why. My mother had been suddenly taken with a fit; in my great anxiety for her dear life I had forgotten the day for writing to Malta. But surely the missing of one post need not have caused you much distress."

"I was only somewhat troubled," continued Oscar; "I thought that my betrothed might be ill, I never thought that she could be false. When the pilot met us in the Channel I made sure of a letter, and was foremost in the throng that crowded to the vessel's side to seize on the contents of his bag. To my great disappointment there was no letter for me in your familiar hand, only one in your cousin's. I tore that open with feverish haste: Walter would tell me whether you were ill, perhaps—as my fears suggested—dying. There were only two lines written in that fatal letter; they were branded on my brain as with burning iron—'*Io is mine; I have won the prize.*'"

"Oh, the poor foolish boy!" exclaimed Io. "He did not tell you that he had given my name to his hunter, and that in a steeple-chase she was first. I remember Walter's saying to me that he had played on you a practical joke."

"A joke which cost the poor fellow his life, and has blasted mine," groaned Oscar. "The jealousy which I had deemed stifled for ever suddenly blazed up within me, till my soul was as a furnace sevenfold heated. When the *Argus* neared Dover pier I sprang out, narrowly missing falling into the sea—spectators must have thought me mad. Would that I had been drowned, and so had never lived to look on him whom I hated! I determined to see you at once, and learn the whole truth from your lips. I hurried along the shortest path, that at the top of the cliffs, so often trodden with you. As I passed on I heard a voice gasp out my name; I saw two hands grasping the ground not two yards from the path, and I saw the head of the climber who had just reached the top of the cliff. The face had the flush caused by violent physical effort, but I deemed it the flush of triumph. It was Walter's face; he had just breath enough left to cry, '*I've won!*' Those were his last words. For a moment I appeared to be possessed by a demon—I was possessed, for I did the deed of which I repented even before I heard the sound of the crash below."

Io hid her face in her hands and shuddered.

"Then on I sped—a second Cain—resolved but on one thing—to see you, to tax you with your perfidy, and then—I knew not what would follow. You met me with open arms and a cry of delight. You know the rest. For me there is memory of nothing but a kind of hideous dream, till—I know not how long afterwards— you laid before me that letter which proved that you had always been true, and that I had been not only a villain but a fool. Io, for some time I felt that I could not offer you a murderer's hand; that I should fly from you and the world. Then your altered circumstances, and your mother's, made me change my mind. I might still give you a husband's protection, more than a husband's love, and you should never know that marriage had linked you to one whom you might justly abhor. Io, do you not hate me?"

Io's only reply was throwing herself on her husband's breast, with her arms clinging round his neck. Oscar's confession, made at cost of so much shame and anguish, made him seem dearer than ever.

"Oscar, I love you, oh so fondly! God loves you too, and He will forgive. Remember the thief on the cross."

"He confessed and found mercy, but it was from a cross," said Oscar Coldstream. "I have not yet taken up mine; I have shunned it—I shun it still."

"What do you mean?" cried Io, raising her head;

"you have confessed, and fully.   You are not a Romanist; you look not for priestly absolution."

"Io, I have not only broken God's law, but the laws of my country.   Justice demands a victim.   My cross is to let the world know my guilt, publicly to confess my crime and accept its penalty, even should it be a death of shame.   Nothing less than this can give to a guilty conscience peace.   You have said that it is your desire —your right—to judge; judge then what course should I take.   I leave the decision in the hands of my wife."

"I cannot judge, I cannot think—my brain turns round," faltered Io, her white lips with difficulty uttering the words, while she pressed her head with both her hands.

"Sahib, all ready for starting."   How strangely the native servant's commonplace announcement broke on the terrible stillness which had followed the exclamation of Io.

Mrs. Coldstream started to her feet.   "Let us go, let us go quickly!" she cried wildly; "let us leave this terrible spot!   I must have time to think—time to pray.   I will give you my answer—*to-morrow!*"

CHAPTER XXII.

HOME AGAIN.

Io's yearning was for quietness and solitude, but in the village neither was now to be found. The Karens, smiling, and with little offerings in their hands, came to see the white travellers start. There were crying babies and laughing children, quiet girls and noisy boys, such as are always to be expected in a mixed crowd. Several women came with their palms pressed together, as if preferring a request. One bowed down almost to the ground, so as to touch the lady's feet. There was a good deal of talking, apparently addressed to Io; but her senses were so bewildered by the late shock, that she could not take in a single word. Io looked helplessly at her husband for an explanation.

"They are begging you to leave Maha with them, my love. The woman says that she has lost her only child, and desires to adopt Maha as her daughter. I have spoken to Ko Thah Byu, who gives to the widow a high character for piety."

The object of the petition was mutely standing by

with her hands clasped, and her dark eyes watching the face of her mistress.

"Does Maha wish to stay here?" asked Io. She spoke in English, and Oscar translated the question.

"These are Karens, mine own people," replied Maha, with a wistful glance at the widow; "and she is so like my dead mother."

"Would it pain you to part with your *protégée*, my Io?" asked Oscar.

"Pain? no, nothing pains now, but—" She paused, and pressed her hand on her heart. Io was somewhat like the poor victim broken on the wheel, who, after the first crushing blow had paralyzed sensation, mocked at the idea of any other stroke having power to hurt.

Oscar hastily completed the arrangement, and then, turning towards Ko Thah Byu, warmly grasped his brown hand.

"You have done much for me—more than you know, my brother," said the Englishman to the Karen. "You have helped to release me from bonds which I believed would have bound me for ever."

It was a relief to the Coldstreams when Mouang was left behind, though Maha and others followed Io's litter for more than a mile, the Karen girl weeping bitterly at parting from the mistress whom she honoured and loved. At length the last farewell was said, and Io felt alone; for Oscar dropped behind the litter, respecting his wife's wish for absolute silence—a wish which, after the excite-

ment of the morning, he fully shared. Io closed her
eyes to shut out all sights, but the mind's eye could not
be closed. The less she saw the more she thought.
The face of poor Walter, her childhood's companion, con-
tinually rose before her! It was some comfort to her
now, as it had been when she had first heard of his
sudden death, that her merry hare-brained young cousin
had had serious thoughts on religion; that with all his
giddiness he had received the truth with the simple
faith of a child. Io would not have had this comfort
had her brother been the one to be suddenly taken.

The halting-place for the night was reached at last,
where the little tent was already pitched, the fire lighted,
the meal prepared. Coldstream avoided any allusion to
painful subjects as he sat beside his pale wife, and helped
her to food which Io in vain attempted to eat. Coldstream related all that he had heard from Ko Thah Byu
of the Karen's former life; and Io, though she made no
comment on the strange tale, readily understood what
influence it had had on the mind of her husband.

The lady early laid herself down to rest, but not to
sleep. Feverish and restless Io remained through what
appeared to be an almost interminable night. If a few
minutes of slumber came, they were rendered horrible
by dreams in which the terrible tragedy of the cliff was
acted over again. But Oscar was able to sleep; his
wife marvelled to see how calmly he rested. The cause
of this was partly physical fatigue and reaction after a

violent inward struggle, but partly that his confession to his wife had in some measure relieved his conscience. He had taken the first step—or rather desperate leap—under the weight of the cross which he had at last dared to take up.

Day dawned, and with it came the morning's preparations, the morning's start.

"Oscar, will you arrange that we do not reach Moulmein till quite after dark?" said Io, as she took her place in the litter. "The moon does not rise now so early. I wish no one to know of our arrival. I could not endure to-day to meet Thud or the doctor."

"There is no fear of our meeting till to-morrow morning," replied Oscar. "All the English residents of Moulmein were invited to spend this Thursday evening at a *fête* given by the rajah."

"Thursday! I thought that this was Saturday," said Io dreamily. "It seems as if this week would never come to an end."

It was not till after dark that the Coldstreams reached their home, where they were expected by no one. All their servants, except one lame old man, had gone to see the rajah's fireworks. No fires were lighted in the compound, no lamp in the dwelling. It was with some difficulty that even the door was opened to receive the master of the house. The furniture was in the holland wrappings in which Io had left her things when expecting to be absent for weeks. It was a dreary coming home, but more congenial to sad feelings than a cheerful greeting would have been.

"I will go to rest at once," said Io. Nature was demanding sleep; after the last two terrible nights the lady could scarcely keep her eyes open.

"Shall we first pray together?" suggested Oscar.

Blessed rift in the dark, dark cloud! Oscar could at last kneel down by the side of his wife and pray aloud. And what a prayer was his! It seemed to be poured out at the feet of a Saviour in visible presence—a pleading, imploring prayer for mercy on the guiltiest of the guilty. But it was a prayer uttered in faith and hope—faith that there is indeed a Fountain to wash away sin; hope that its stain had already been removed from a penitent's soul. The sinner was prostrate indeed, but, like Saul of Tarsus, in deep humility, not in despair. Io drank in each word of the prayer. It refreshed her, it strengthened her, while it made her tears flow fast. When the supplication was ended, the "Amen" came from her lips with a sob.

Then the husband and wife arose from their knees. Oscar knew that the mail for Calcutta would start on the morrow, and Io had promised to give her answer on the day which had now passed into night.

"What would you have me do now, my beloved?" Oscar inquired, taking the hand of his wife.

Io knew what he meant. "Whatever you think right," was the faltered reply.

The husband pressed a long, tender kiss on Io's cold brow.   Not another word passed between them.   Io went to her own room, and Coldstream retired to his study.

Seated in that study, Oscar wrote a brief but full account of his crime in an official letter addressed to Government House.   He omitted nothing, except the cause of the hatred which he owned that he had felt towards his unfortunate victim; he made not the slightest reference to his wife.   Oscar wrote with a strange calmness which was to himself a matter of surprise. He then lighted a taper and sealed up his document, placed it in his desk, which he locked, read awhile in his Bible, and then retired to rest.

CHAPTER XXIII.

AN ORDEAL.

OSCAR arose very early, before his wife was awake. He went to his study, and, after long fervent prayer, took out the large sealed letter and carried it himself to the post. The postmaster was making up the bag for the Calcutta mail, whistling a light air as he did so. Oscar gave in the letter with a hand that did not tremble, and turned away with the thought, "I *have* plucked out the right eye."

Coldstream did not at once direct his steps homewards. He went first to a kind of warehouse with a deep veranda half filled up with advertisements on placards, pieces of second-hand furniture too large to be stowed inside, empty packing-cases, and other articles of a heterogeneous nature. This was the establishment of Hersey the agent, who monopolized most of the custom of the European residents in Moulmein. The proprietor, seated in the veranda, was taking his morning cup of coffee before business hours should commence.

Mr. Coldstream was well known to Hersey, who had

procured for that gentleman most of the furniture of
his house. Hersey rose, put down his cup, raised his
hat, and wished Mr. Coldstream good-morning. He
offered Oscar a seat, but his offer was declined. Mr.
Coldstream preferred standing.

Much astonished was Hersey when he found on what
business his early visitor had come, when Coldstream
informed the agent that he wished to put his dwelling,
with all its fittings, into his hands for sale in the following month.

Hersey expressed his surprise. He could hardly believe that Mr. Coldstream could really intend to dispose
of the house prepared at the cost of much labour and
expense, which was generally acknowledged to be the
one best fitted up in the station.

"It is my wish to sell it furnished," said Mr. Coldstream. "My wife and I are about to quit Moulmein."

"I am sure, sir, we shall be very sorry to lose you,"
said Hersey.

After settling this affair, Coldstream, with a quick
step—for he wished to get over painful business as
rapidly as he might—proceeded to his own office, which
opened on the wharf. Coldstream, as he expected, found
Smith overlooking labourers at work in the extensive
yard which adjoined the premises. There were some
repairs going on, and the sound of hammer and saw rose
in the morning air. Smith respectfully greeted his

chief, and made a remark on the work on which the labourers were employed.

"A fine bit of timber that, Mr. Coldstream ; one does not see such every day," he observed.

"No ; the tree must have been a grand one before it fell beneath the axe," said Oscar.—"Smith, come with me to the office ; I have some matters which I wish to talk over with you there."

The two men were soon seated in the office. Smith, a shrewd, intelligent man of business, thoroughly master of his work, listened with unfeigned surprise to a proposal made by his employer by which his own position in life would be entirely changed. The reader need not be troubled by details. Coldstream's plan, matured during his long pedestrian journey, was to make over his whole business to a man who had twice managed it satisfactorily during his own absence. An agreement would have to be drawn up by a lawyer by which Smith would engage to pay a certain yearly sum to Mrs. Coldstream as interest on the capital which his former employer had sunk in the business. The offer was a liberal one, and its acceptance would at once place Smith in a position to which he had never hoped to attain.

"But, my dear sir, Mr. Coldstream, why should you give up the business ?" cried Smith. "You are in the prime of life ; thoroughly master of the work. I have served you, and your respected father before you, for more than twenty years. I never looked even to partner-ship; and now you would place everything in my hands! I hope that your health is not failing—nothing the matter with your heart." The honest man looked with affectionate anxiety at the pale, worn face of his chief, that anxiety mitigating but not destroying the pleasure which he naturally felt at the prospect of his own ad-vancement.

"It is not want of health that takes me from Moul-mein," replied Oscar.

"But you will return, my dear sir—you will certainly return and take up the business again? I will act under your orders and in your name, as I have twice done when you were absent in England."

Mr. Coldstream shook his head gravely. "No, Smith; I wish to make an arrangement definite—final. I shall never return to Moulmein." Then, after a pause, he went on: "I have one other stipulation to make, though it cannot be put into legal form like the arrangement in favour of Mrs. Coldstream. I must add the condition that you give employment at a moderate salary to her brother, young Thorn, who has come to Moulmein in the hope of finding some means of earning his living."

Smith raised his eyebrows and shrugged his shoulders a little. Something like a smile came to his lips.

"I willingly agree to take the young master into the business," said he, "and give him a sufficient salary, with prospect of increase; but I cannot engage to keep him on unless he shows himself willing to work. Master Thorn is so desirous to instruct, that I find it uncommonly hard to get him to learn ; and we can't get into any profession by jumping over the wall—we must take the trouble of opening the gate."

"Do you think the lad deficient in intellect?" inquired Mr. Coldstream.

"Oh dear, no, sir! he has as much brain as most other boys; only he thinks that he has a thousand times more," replied Smith with a grin. "Master Thorn is lazy too, he is; he ought to have been at his work here more than an hour ago."

"I see him coming; I will go and meet him. I will tell him of our arrangement, and say that you agree to give him a trial."

"Yes, sir, a trial. I'll do what I can, for your sake and the lady's; but Master Thorn should know that the result must depend on his own behaviour."

"Young Thorn needs the spur of necessity," observed Mr. Coldstream; "he may do better when we are away." Then, bidding Smith good-morning, Oscar quitted the office, and went with quick step to meet Thud, who was approaching with a slow one.

"Why—I say—you back already! I did not expect you for a fortnight!" exclaimed Thud. The lad's heavy face showed signs of the effect of the festival of the last evening; his cheeks were more puffed and his eyes a little more blinking than usual.

"We met with an adventure," replied Oscar, "and both Io and I decided to return at once. Besides, I have many arrangements to make. We **are** going to leave Moulmein."

"Oh, I am glad of that!" cried Thud. "It's the most stupid place under the sun; it has not so much as a **club-room or a museum.** When shall we start?"

"It is **not a case** of *we*," replied Mr. Coldstream; "I am compelled to leave you behind in Moulmein."

"I won't stay behind when you go," said Thud bluntly.

"I **am afraid** that **you will** hardly have a choice," replied **his** brother-in-law; and Oscar explained to Thud the arrangement which he had made for his benefit, and tried to show him how much to his advantage it was to be received at once as a paid assistant, instead of being simply apprenticed.

"*I*—an assistant to that low fellow Smith, the son of a London tailor!" exclaimed Thud, with intense disgust.

"No matter whose **son he** may be; he is a good, honest, sensible man, who **has** worked his own way up in the world. **Mr.** Smith **is** the only person whom I know willing to give you such a chance."

"I'll go with you. Where are you going?" asked Thud.

"Where we go is not the **question**; I have told you already that you cannot go with us."

Thud ground his teeth in anger. "I'll return to England at once," growled he.

"Who will pay for your passage? I certainly shall not," said Oscar. "Listen, my boy," he continued, laying his hand in a kindly way on the shoulder of Thud. "I believe that the separation will be for your good. Thrown on your own resources, you will show what mettle is in you; you will learn to work so as to be a help to a widowed mother, and not a burden. You have an opportunity of redeeming the time; the ball is at your foot—"

Thud showed what he was likely to do with the symbolical ball by violently kicking a large stone which lay in the way, to the detriment of his boot and the bruising of the foot which it covered.

"Think over the matter," said Oscar. "I tell you again that I have done for you the best that I possibly can. Now go to your work; I have business elsewhere."

Thud did not go to his work; he was in a violent passion, partially restrained before Oscar, but about to burst in full fury on Io. Hurrying home, Thud found his sister buried in painful thought; for she felt certain that the letter of terrible import had been sent—that her husband had done what was right, facing results that might be fearful. Thud never noticed his sister's distressed looks, never greeted her after her absence, but burst like a tornado upon her.

"I say, Oscar has behaved shamefully—disgracefully

—brutally!" exclaimed the lad, his short hair appearing to bristle up with anger.

Io started to her feet in alarm. Was it possible that Thud knew the fatal secret—that he was speaking of Walter's death by her husband's hand? The next sentence sputtered forth reassured her on this point at least.

"He has lured me here to this detestable place by promising to find me occupation, as a rat is lured into a trap by cheese; and so he has caught me, and I cannot get out. Oscar has treated me abominably! *I*—Thucydides Thorn—*I* an assistant to the son of a tailor! I'd sooner be sewn up in a sack and thrown into the sea!"

Io tried her utmost to soothe her brother. She appealed to his love for his mother, his love for herself; she tried to touch on motives higher still. But even her winning gentleness had little or no effect. Thud was indignant at Io's refusing to promise to use all her influence to induce Oscar to change his mind. He called her conduct unnatural and unkind. The interview was to the half broken-hearted Io like vinegar on a fresh wound. She was almost relieved to see Mrs. Cottle's short, thick figure coming bustling up the path, for she knew that Thud would avoid meeting one who laughed at him more mercilessly than did Dr. Pinfold himself. Mrs. Cottle had never before ventured to call before breakfast, and her company was far from congenial to Io; but it was something that her approach closed the conversation which was becoming painful almost beyond endurance. Thud went off in high dudgeon to pour out the tale of his wrongs to Pogson. The poor dog was indeed being thrown into the water to teach him to swim, and great was the splash and the struggle.

Mrs. Cottle had been too full of eager curiosity to wait for the visiting-hour. She was glad to catch Io in the veranda, giving the poor lady no time to retreat into the house.

"My dear, dear Mrs. Coldstream," cried the visitor, taking both of Io's hands and shaking them with unusual warmth of manner. "Goodness me, how ill you look! and one cannot wonder at it. What is it that I hear? I dropped in early at Hersey's to look at the screen which he has for sale, and he told me—but I'm sure that it cannot be true—that Mr. Coldstream is going to carry you off, and sell this beautiful house!"

"Please sit down, Mrs. Cottle," said poor Io, releasing her hands from her visitor's grasp, but unable to avoid the gaze of her peering, curious eyes.

Mrs. Cottle plumped down on a chair, and made it crack with her weight. Io also seated herself, for she was hardly able to stand. . .

"Only tell me, my dear, that this shocking rumour is not true," cried Mrs. Cottle.

"It is true that we must quit Moulmein," said Io sadly; "and of course Mr. Coldstream will part with the house."

"Such a beauty! green poplin furniture—curtains to

match—pictures, mirrors!" cried Mrs. Cottle, glancing around, the idea of auction-sale and cheap bargains flitting through her mind. "My dear, you must make a stand—you must persuade; and if persuasion won't do, must resist."

"I never resist my husband's will," replied Io, an indignant flush giving a brief colour to her pale cheek.

"That's it," said Mrs. Cottle; "you're much too soft. Men love to play the tyrant and lord it over the meek Griseldas. We all see what you suffer."

"Mrs. Cottle, I am not accustomed to such language, and I will not bear it!" cried Io, rising from her seat. "I have the best, the kindest of husbands, and would willingly go with him to the end of the world!" Unable to bear the conversation longer, Io made a hasty apology to her visitor, and retreated into the house.

"Ah, that's what always happens," said Mrs. Cottle to herself, as she went on her way. "You can't come between a man and his wife. If he were beating her to death, and you interfered, she would tell you to go about your business. But I'm sorry for that poor, silly girl! I always said that she had made a dreadful mistake in marrying a gloomy tyrant like Coldstream."

Mrs. Cottle went to comfort herself for the briefness of her interview with Io by talking over the miseries of a woman wedded to a Bluebeard with every gossip in the station.

Even in her home, shut up in her own room to be

more safe from intrusion, Io was not to be left to herself. Presently Dr. Pinfold's loud voice resounded through the dwelling.

"Io, my dear, where are you? I've come to see you," cried the doctor, the visitor who could never be shut out. Even had his god-daughter been ill in her bed, that would not have excluded the medical man. Io screwed up her courage as best she might, and came forth to greet her old friend, heartily wishing herself back in the solitude of the woods.

"Bless me, my child, what's the matter?" exclaimed Pinfold, with real concern, when his favourite made her appearance. "You look like a criminal going to be hanged!" Io winced at the terrible word. "You are trembling like an aspen, my girl. What on earth has pulled you down thus?"

Io made a desperate effort to smile and assume a cheerful manner, as she made her old friend sit down on the sofa beside her. "Dear Dr. Pinny, shall I relate some of our adventures?" she said. "First, poor Thud fell from the tat—"

"And lost his teeth and his beauty," laughed Pinfold. "He wanted me to put the teeth in again; but I told him that they could only be put into a museum."

Io was well pleased at having diverted attention from her own looks. She then, with a desperate energy which surprised herself, went on to give a description of the alarming night-adventure—Oscar knocked down,

seized, and bound to a tree; she herself in the hands of
the Shans.   Her vivid description elicited many an exclamation from the old doctor.

"I thought that a pleasure-trip would do you good,"
cried the kind-hearted man; "but it seems that I was
pouring vitriol down my patient's throat to serve as a
tonic! I never bargained for savages and robbers. I
hope that Coldstream gave the fellow who saved you a
handsome present. And now you must try to forget
your fright—or write a novel about it; and you must
be well nourished up—*àpropos* to which the savoury
scent from the dining-room tells me that our breakfast
is ready."

Io was not sorry, under the circumstances, that business had delayed Oscar's return, and that he, at least,
would not have to eat his breakfast under the eye of
the doctor.

"By-the-by," said Pinfold, as he poured the hot milk
on the *suji*, "what means this nonsensical report about
your and your husband's leaving Moulmein?"

How often had the Coldstreams to endure the ordeal
of such questions during the next few days! They almost
dreaded the sight of a European visitor, except that of
the chaplain, who had too much consideration to show
curiosity. Had there not been so much business to be
settled, so many arrangements to make, the Coldstreams
would have tried to escape from daily annoyance by
making a second excursion.

"One comfort **is** that to-morrow the English ship comes in," thought Io, after **a** day **of** peculiar vexation. "I shall have the luxury of **a nice** long letter from my darling mother, who knows nothing **yet of our trouble.** It will contain some **loving token for Christmas,** which is now so near, **and interesting particulars of dear** Jane's engagement, **only** briefly mentioned **in the last letters.** In news from my loved **English home I** shall find some comfort still."

CHAPTER XXIV.

CHRISTMAS.

THE mail came, but not the comfort. The only letter was a black-edged one addressed to Oscar. He came to his wife with the letter open in his hand, and sadly and tenderly broke to her its contents. A fit, resembling that which had attacked Mrs. Thorn in the early part of the year, had this time proved fatal. Jane wrote to her brother-in-law from the chamber in which lay a dear form in the stillness of death.

Many tears did Io shed over the letter; and yet both to her and to Oscar there came a mournful consolation in the thought that the gentle lady had been saved from knowledge of the cause of the frightful death of her nephew Walter, her sister's orphan child, whom she had brought up with her own. The dark shadow over Io's home would throw no blackness over her mother's grave.

Thud's grief for the loss of his parent was shown in more violent form than Io's. He flung himself on the sofa, and cried and howled like a passionate child. There was no small admixture of selfishness in the sorrow of the poor lad. He had lost a home as well as a parent, and had now no resource to fall back upon when he needed money or help. Thud realized at last that he *must* swim by his own exertions, unless he intended to sink. There was in Thud at least a temporary improvement; for a while he built up no fanciful theories, obtruded on others no foolish opinions, and quietly went to his work. Io earnestly hoped that the vain lad would grow up at last into the useful, sensible man.

There was a change also in Oscar, apparent in manner and mien, and shown in his countenance, which was grave but no longer gloomy. A deep peace had followed confession. No cloud hid the brightness of the Saviour's face from the penitent sinner. Oscar had committed a crime, and was prepared to bear its penalty; but it would be in this world and not in the next. Coldstream was at last in the position of the thief on the cross: the criminal saw the blood flowing for his salvation, and heard in his heart the voice speaking in mercy and love, "Thou, even thou, shalt be in paradise with Me."

Especially did Oscar realize the blessing on him whose transgression is pardoned when he attended divine service on Christmas day. Io had given orders that every bud and blossom should be stripped from her garden to adorn the church. She had not had heart to join in the work herself; but when the Coldstreams entered the building, the soft fragrance around reminded them of the ointment poured forth on the Saviour's feet from the broken box of alabaster. Husband and wife each brought a broken and contrite heart; both knew that it was for such that the Lord of glory had come to earth.

At a later hour in the day, Oscar, when taking a solitary walk, was joined by the chaplain. Mark Lawrence had noticed with deep interest and hope the change in the expression of the face of his friend. He had observed something like hesitation in the manner of Coldstream before he turned away to quit the church in which his wife stayed to Communion. The heart of the young clergyman yearned with a brother's love over his friend. With some hope that Oscar might at length speak freely, Lawrence came on that Christmas afternoon to his side. To the chaplain's satisfaction, Coldstream was the first to break silence on the subject uppermost in the minds of both.

"I did not turn my back to-day on the holy table because I thought that my Lord would forbid my approach," said Coldstream in a quiet tone. "I believe that the feast is spread for the prodigal son, and that even I would be welcomed now to the Father's table. I kept back on account of others, because, when that is known which must soon be known, communicants might be scandalized and shocked to think that they had shared the cup of blessing with a criminal such as I am."

Lawrence was silent. He was of too delicate a mind by a single word to hasten on a confession. Coldstream passed on to a somewhat different subject.

"In another world how think you that a Paul would meet with a Stephen, a Manasseh with Isaiah, David with the man whom he had foully wronged, deceived, and slain?"

"I think that all the redeemed will meet as brethren in the Father's home," replied Lawrence; "there the most deeply injured will forgive."

Oscar gave a sigh, but it was as much a sigh of relief as of sorrow.

"And do you believe," said he, "that amongst those whose robes are washed white the bitterness of remorse for crimes committed on earth will not remain to taint even the bliss of heaven?"

"I believe, my dear friend, that God having blotted out all sin as a cloud is blotted from the sky, leaving no stain behind, no grief will remain, but only more fervent gratitude from those who have had the heaviest debt. Those whom Christ saves are justified, those who are justified are glorified too; no blot can rest on the beams of those who shine like the sun."

"Thanks," said Coldstream earnestly; "and may I hope that even when you know what a sinner you have called your 'dear friend,' you will still retain some kindly, indulgent feeling towards him?"

"I will never feel anything but warm friendship

towards you whatever you may have done," cried Mark Lawrence.

With these words, and a warm press of the hand, the two men separated, for their paths lay in different directions. The brief conversation with Oscar often recurred to the mind of Lawrence, even when he sat at a festal Christmas board, with lively talk going on around.

"If my conjecture be correct," reflected the chaplain, "Coldstream has killed some man in a duel, and has bitterly repented of the deed."

CHAPTER XXV.

FAREWELL.

IT need not be said that the Coldstreams awaited with more than interest the important reply to Oscar's letter, though they never spoke about it. There were but two mails in the course of each week. Carefully had the days been calculated the lapse of which would render an acknowledgment of Coldstream's confession possible. Communication between different stations in the East was comparatively slow in the time of King William.

The first day on which a reply from Calcutta could be expected was the day after Christmas. It was not without emotion that the letter-bag was opened by Coldstream. Was it a disappointment or a relief to find in it nothing but a newspaper and a note from a tradesman? Io, in a fever of anxiety, had stolen into the room to learn if the dreaded despatch had come. The question was asked only in a look, and a slight shake of the head was the silent reply.

Coldstream had made every arrangement for quitting Moulmein after the second Calcutta mail should arrive.

He had taken a passage for his wife and himself in a schooner which was to start on the noon of the day when the mail would be due: better, he thought, to run the risk of forfeiting the passage money than that of having to remain in Moulmein four days after his crime should be publicly known there. Io had everything prepared for a start.

The next mail came on a Tuesday, the last Tuesday of the year. Io watched the opening of the bag, and gasped with agitation as a large official despatch with a Government seal was drawn forth. Oscar lifted up his heart in silent prayer before he broke that seal.

The document was couched in stiff official language. Mr. Coldstream's communication was acknowledged. As the affair had occurred in England, the case would be referred to the authorities at home, where doubtless a record of the inquest held on the body of Mr. Walter Manly had been preserved. Until directions should be received from England, Mr. Coldstream was required to surrender his person to the police authorities in Calcutta.

"Mine own! mine own! I will share your imprisonment," cried Io, pressing her husband's hand to her lips.

"No, my love; you will live near, and obtain permission to visit me often," said Oscar. "We will await the final decision from England with faith, patience, and submission. And now, is all ready for our start?"

"We have not bidden good-bye to poor Thud," said Io; "I have not seen him to-day."

"No; I sent him off to the office as soon as he had had his early breakfast. As Thud is close to the wharf, he will come to see us off ere the vessel starts. We wish no prolonged good-byes."

It is not a matter of wonder that when final arrangements had to be made, the keys of the house placed in the agent's hands, and the inventory looked over, the Calcutta newspaper which had arrived that morning should lie unopened on the table, beside the packets of groceries and such like things that had been prepared for the voyage. But other copies of that newspaper had reached Moulmein, and had not been equally neglected. One was in the hands of Mrs. Cottle as she was sitting at breakfast with her husband. Being busily occupied with his fried fish and anchovy sauce, Cottle had deferred the perusal of the paper, and left his wife to look out first for the paragraphs of gossip and scandal which were to her the sauce to a dry dish of politics and statistics.

"Bless my heart! bless my heart! *bless my heart!*" exclaimed Mrs. Cottle, each repetition of the blessing made in a louder and more emphatic tone, which roused the attention of her spouse.

"What is it, my dear?" quoth Cottle.

"I always knew it; I always said it. He was no fit company for us, the hypocritical, sneaking, bloodthirsty villain."

"Who is it, my dear?" asked Cottle, laying down his knife and fork to listen with more undivided attention.

"Here is a paragraph—look; it is easy enough to make out its meaning," cried Mrs. Cottle, and with terrible emphasis she read aloud from the paper :—

"MURDER BY A GENTLEMAN.—It is reported that a Mr. C—— of M——n has confessed to having killed, by throwing down a cliff, a person against whom he had a grudge. As Mr. C—— is said to be of very good family, with high connections, the case is likely to excite great interest in England amongst the upper ten thousand."

"But we are not of the upper ten thousand, so what is it to us?" said honest John Cottle.

"We know Mr. Coldstream, and it must be he!" cried his partner; "M——n must stand for Moulmein."

"It might stand for Moultan or Macedon," quoth Cottle. "And C is a common letter enough; it might stand for my name."

"What nonsense you talk!" cried his irreverent spouse. "C—— is Coldstream, and M——n Moulmein; it does not need two grains of sense to understand that."

Cottle put on his glasses, and stretched out his hand for the paper. Mrs. Cottle, as she poured out the coffee, again exclaimed, "Bless my heart!"

After breakfast was concluded the dame sallied forth to communicate the exciting news to others. The first person whom she chanced to meet was the chaplain.

"O Mr. Lawrence, have you seen the horrible news about Mr. Coldstream?" she cried, hoping that she might be the first person to impart it to the clergyman.

"I have seen the papers," said Mark very gravely. He wished to pass on, but Mrs. Cottle was determined to have out her say.

"To think of such a wretch kneeling in the same church as ourselves! A felon having the audacity to dine with respectable people!"

Mrs. Cottle would have rattled on, but she was stopped by the sternest rebuke which she had ever heard from the lips of the chaplain: "Judge not, that ye be not judged; condemn not, lest ye be condemned." And with these words Mark Lawrence went on his way, his brow knitted as if from pain, and a heavy weight on his heart.

The paragraph in the papers had also been read by Dr. Pinfold, as he was lounging in his easy-chair before going out to make his round amongst his patients. He had perused a column and a half of political news before his eye was attracted by the paragraph headed in large capitals which had at once arrested the attention of Mrs. Cottle. Pinfold's interest in Io was much stronger than hers, and, though less loudly expressed, his indignation against her husband was proportionately greater.

"The villain! and he dared to propose marriage to *her*; to offer the sweetest girl in England a blood-stained hand!" exclaimed the doctor, flinging down the paper and rising from his seat. "I suspected him of being a madman; I never thought of his being a murderer. My poor Io! innocent, unfortunate victim, if I can I will rescue you yet."

So as Io, just about to quit her house, was buttoning on her boots, a servant placed a letter on the table before her.

"It is from dear old Pinny; I know his handwriting. Please read it to me, Oscar. I thought that the doctor had bidden us his final good-bye last night."

Oscar opened the letter, looked surprised at its contents, and, without comment, handed it on to his wife. The doctor's scrawl ran thus:—

"MY DEAR CHILD,—I always thought your marriage a mistake, but I never knew till now what a great one. You must not think of sacrificing yourself by accompanying your miserable husband. His conduct cancels all obligations entered into through ignorance of the truth. I offer you a home here in Moulmein. You are my god-child, the daughter of my old friend; I will adopt you as my own. Whilst I live you shall find a parent in your old Pinny."

Io flushed with indignation as she read; then tore the letter into minute fragments, and trampled them under her foot.

"It was kindly meant," observed Oscar.

" What ! to insult you to your own wife ! to en-
deavour to divide me from you ! O Oscar, Oscar, how
little he knows me ! I would rather never see daylight
again than be separated from my husband ! "

" Then let us now go on our way," said Oscar, " and
meet trial and misfortune together. Your palanquin
waits outside."

Io silently entered it. She put down the curtains on
either side as she started for the place of embarkation,
that no one might see her tear-bedewed face. Oscar
walked to the docks, but by a round-about route
amongst low narrow lanes, frequented only by natives.
He pulled his hat over his brow, and never raised his
eyes from the path before him, for the doctor's letter
had shown to him plainly that his secret was a secret no
longer. Coldstream's circuitous route brought him to
the docks a little after his wife. His arrival interrupted a distressing conversation which she was having with Thud, who was making a last desperate
attempt to persuade his sister to take him with her
to Calcutta.

" You know that mother would never have treated
me so," cried the lad ; " now she is gone, and you desert
me. It is cruel, it is unnatural ! it is because you are
such a slave to—" Here Thud suddenly paused, for
Coldstream was at his side.

" Farewell, Thud," said Oscar, holding out his hand.
" Do your duty to man and to God, and may He prosper

and bless you.—Io, my love, enough of this; the sooner we are on board the better."

The Coldstreams were soon treading the deck of the *Dolphin*, but the plank which connected the vessel with the shore was not yet raised. Smith came to see his friend and benefactor depart, and again express hopes of his happy return. Smith had not seen the newspapers; he never read them till business hours were over.

"Would that we were fairly off!" thought Oscar; but another good-bye was before him yet ere the keel of the *Dolphin* should plough the green waves.

"Ah, Mr. Lawrence!" exclaimed Io.

The chaplain crossed the plank, pale with suppressed emotion. He walked up straight to Oscar, and took his hand in both his own.

"You know all, and yet you do not turn from me," said Oscar.

"I have come to give you my parting blessing—to unite with you, perhaps for the last time, in prayer." The chaplain could scarcely command his voice as he added, "I honour you for having done all that you could do to—" Here Mark Lawrence fairly broke down; he could not finish the sentence.

"Clear boards. You'd better be off, sir, unless you mean to make the voyage with us," said the captain of the *Dolphin* gruffly. "We're weighing anchor, you see."

There was no more time for conversation, for nothing but cordial pressure of hands. The plank was raised the minute after **Mark** Lawrence had **passed over. The** wind swelled the sails, **and the vessel moved on, leaving** a brief track **on the waters behind her.**

"Even as those **bubbles on the waves will earth's** darkest trials **pass away," thought the chaplain as he** watched the departing **ship. "There goes a man who is** as a gallant vessel **that has suddenly struck on a rock** and been **almost wrecked, that has all but sunk below** the **billows, but which, through God's grace, has been** given power **to rise above them. Its cargo of earthly** reputation **and earthly joy is indeed lost; but it is** bravely struggling **on, though with torn sail and shat-** tered mast, **towards that port where the rock cannot** crush nor the tempest **toss, where the pardoned penitent** finds peace **for ever."**

Mark **Lawrence turned homewards, repeating to him-** self the well-known verse :—

> " Though tempest-torn, and half a wreck,
> My Saviour through the floods I seek ;
> Let neither wind nor stormy main
> Force back my shattered bark again ! "

CHAPTER XXVI.

PRISON LIFE.

"THIS is the last day of the year," observed Io to her husband, when they stood together on the deck as the vessel, sailing up the muddy Hoogly after a very rapid voyage, neared the city of palaces—"the last day of the year which begun with such hope and joy."

"And closes with such sorrow," thought Oscar. Husband and wife each silently revolved the question, "What will the new year bring?"

"Even what God will," was the answer in Coldstream's heart. "The worst is over, and I can peacefully await whatever He may send."

The new year began to Oscar within the walls of a prison, but he was subjected to no rigorous confinement. The man who had been his own accuser was treated as a gentleman by the officials; was allowed a separate cell, and permitted to receive daily visits from his wife. Io would have entreated to be allowed to share the cell, but Oscar forbade her making any such application. A quiet home was found for the poor young wife in a missionary's dwelling, situated not very far from the prison; and every morning a palanquin might be seen going from that house in the direction of the gloomy building which held all that Io loved best upon earth; every day a slight form, dressed in deep mourning, passed through its stern archway. Io heard the heavy bolts drawn behind her, and glided, under the jailer's escort, along the dreary passages which none so fair and innocent as she had ever trodden before. Something of the spirit of a Gertrude von Wart was in the bosom of Io. In a yet more terrible trial she could have said from her inmost soul,—

> " Hath the world aught for me to fear
>   When death is on thy brow?
> The world—what means it? mine is *here*,
>   I will not leave thee now."

But the long hours spent daily by Io in her husband's cell were by no means hours of unmitigated grief. Oscar's calmness had an effect upon the spirit of his wife, naturally so buoyant and cheerful. It was a real pleasure to Io to sit beside her husband whilst he read aloud to her, for books were not denied him. Sometimes Io would write to Oscar's dictation—a privilege which she highly prized. The prisoner found congenial occupation in composing short meditations on the fifty-first psalm. Each day brought its verse for prayerful reflection, and each verse seemed to contain exactly the spiritual food which the penitent's spirit required. *De-*

liver me from blood-guiltiness, **O Lord!** found a strong echo in the prisoner's soul, while the broken and contrite heart drank in with thanksgiving the assurance that it was not despised **even by a** perfectly holy God. Io, by **Oscar's permission,** sent these meditations to the press, and they were **read with profit** by many who little imagined that **they had** been penned in a prison.

Even **hymns of praise, where** two voices blended in humble **thanksgiving, arose from** Coldstream's cell. Criminals confined near it listened **and** wondered, and the **head jailer** declared that he thought that God's **angels** had **begun to visit the prison.** Oscar was no longer in darkness, **though he was rather in** twilight **than in sunshine; not the** evening twilight, resembling **sweet memories of a happy day** passed away, but rather the **early twilight of hope, after** a gloomy starless night, **seen before the full** glory bursts forth in the Eastern sky.

By her **husband's express desire, Io wrote** a letter to **Dr.** Pinfold, thanking him for kindness shown in **old** days, and **not** containing **any** allusion to the offer made by **him which** had given so much pain to the wife. **Io** also wrote repeatedly **to her** brother. But neither **her** letters **to Thud nor** that addressed **to Dr.** Pinfold ever received a reply. The Coldstreams were uneasy about the youth whom they had left at Moulmein, and at length made **inquiries** regarding him **from** Smith, his employer. The reply received was unsatisfactory. For some weeks young Thorn had worked fairly well under constant supervision ; but as soon as he had received his first month's salary, Thud had thrown up his situation as one unworthy of his merits, and had started off for Rangoon. Here all trace of the lad was lost. Letters sent to Rangoon were returned by the dead-letter office ; nothing was known of him to whom they had been addressed. Io was never to find out what had become of her brother. In the ensuing chapter, however, the reader will find information regarding the career of Thucydides Thorn.

CHAPTER XXVII.

ADVENTURES OF AN OWL.

No one had expressed more indignation at Coldstream's crime than did Thud when the news of it reached him. The lad had never liked his brother-in-law, of whom he had stood in some awe. Oscar had never appreciated Thud's wisdom, had sometimes rebuked him, and had actually compelled him to work! Thud revenged himself now by calling Coldstream a disgrace to the family, and declaring that he would never have intercourse either with him or his wife. Thud destroyed two kind letters which he received from Io, and scorned to send a reply. The manner in which the youth spoke of Coldstream roused the indignation of Smith, who was loyal to his old employer, and who called Thud to his face an ungrateful puppy. It is not to be wondered at that Master Thucydides Thorn soon quitted Moulmein.

Nor did he stay long at Rangoon. Thud did little there beyond selling his watch to enable him to go to another place. We will not follow him in all his wanderings. The poor lad travelled far and wide in search of a field for his talents, but never seemed to light on the right one. Thud wore out his stockings, he wore out his shoes, and he utterly wore out his patience. Sometimes Master Thucydides Thorn had to carry a porter's burden before he could eat a dinner. Though his proud spirit rose against begging, more than once Thud was driven to beg; but even in this he had but slender success. Was it the world's fault or that of Thucydides Thorn that one with his talents should be driven to such pitiful straits? Certainly the youth laid the blame on the former, as many proud, foolish sluggards have done before. The world was blind, hard, and senseless; it had kept a Worcester in prison, and persecuted a Galileo.

For nearly two years this struggle with poverty went on. Thud had grown thinner, sadder, and ten years older in appearance; but all his sufferings had not overcome the conceit and self-confidence which had been fostered in him from childhood.

At length, in one of the largest cities of India, Thud found himself, as he thought, favoured by fortune, for he looked not up to a Higher Power. Lingering sadly outside the gate of a kind of zoological garden, more hungry than the wild beasts within, Thud's eye fell on the following advertisement fixed on the wall: *Wanted a keeper who has some knowledge of animals and experience in managing them.* Thud's experience was of a very limited character, but he believed his knowledge to be immense.   Thud at once went to the manager, and presented himself to him as a candidate for the office of keeper.

The manager was a sickly man, with a yellow complexion which told of liver complaint.   Mr. Blane was very impatient indeed to escape for a while to a cooler place ; but the death of one of his keepers, and the dismissal of another for having helped himself systematically from grain provided for birds under his charge, had made it impossible for the manager to get even a few days' respite from work, however urgently needed.

When Thud entered the room of Mr. Blane, the manager was by no means favourably impressed by the appearance of the candidate for the situation of keeper, and was at first disposed to bid the ragged, hunger-pinched young man go about his business.   But when Blane gave Thud a hearing, the manager began to think that to send him off summarily might be a mistake. Young Thorn had natural history at the end of his fingers : he talked of feline, canine, and equine, carnivorous, granivorous, and omnivorous as familiarly as household words ; he declared with such an air of conviction that he could find ways of feeding animals and keeping them healthy at half the usual cost, that Blane began to hope what he desired—that he had lighted on a treasure. The manager asked Thud for his credentials ; of course none could be produced.   Thud said that he was an unfortunate gentleman of good family, who had come to

Moulmein to make scientific researches, and had found, like many others, that it was harder for a philosopher to earn his living there than it was for a coolie.

Mr. Blane then inquired his visitor's name.

"Thucydides Thorn," replied Thud, with an assumed dignity which comically contrasted with the torn state of his jacket, and his shoeless, stockingless, blistered feet.

"Thorn! why, my grandmother was a Thorn," cried Blane, "and it is not a common surname. What part of England do you hail from, my man?"

Then followed a catechising about family names, dates, and places of residence, from which the manager found out, without possibility of mistake, that he saw a second cousin once removed in the poor barefoot gentleman before him.

This was a delightful discovery for Thud, and was scarcely less pleasant to Blane, who shook his cousin heartily by the hand, and, without further inquiry, installed him in office. Thud was at once clothed in Blane's left-off garments, given his second pair of boots, and invited to share his dinner. The half-famished young man was disposed to do full justice to the best repast of which he had partaken since leaving Moulmein. After dinner, Thud was introduced by Blane to the limited collection of birds, beasts, and reptiles under his charge.

"They have been dying off pretty fast lately," ob-

served Blane; "the last keeper embezzled money given
for their food. The lion (alias *cheetah*) did not get the
lion's share."

"Of course you have preserved and stuffed the skins,"
quoth Thud.

"Yes, yes; we've more stuffed creatures now than
live ones, and they give less trouble," observed Blane.
"You see this building to the right? That is our little
museum."

Museum! the word was nectar to Thud. The bright
vision rose before him of a day when he should be not
only keeper but manager—nay, more, proprietor—of
a museum, filled not merely with stuffed monkeys and
snakes, but with all the curiosities of the East.

That evening Mr. Blane started for his too long
deferred holiday trip, which illness obliged him to
prolong from days to weeks.

Thud was at first in his glory, monarch of all he surveyed, "lord of the fowl and the brute." But troubles
will come even to scientific keepers of Zoological Gardens.
A theory of Thud's, that carnivorous beasts may be
trained to thrive on boiled grain, when worked out did
not prove a success. Thud wondered why animals, even
when scientifically treated, would sicken and die. They
seemed to do so on purpose to spite him.

The young philosopher felt a great want of companions. The Gardens had few visitors, and those
visitors did not appreciate Thucydides Thorn, or the

theories which he was always eager to propound. Thud was almost thrown for society on a one-eyed discharged soldier, who now, as a porter, kept the gate. This man, Colin Champer, was discovered by Thud to be a remarkably shrewd, intelligent man. Champer won this character because he was a good listener; he echoed every wise saying dropped by Thud, having no imagination of his own, and gave implicit credence to whatever his oracle said.

One day, after being for some time buried in thought, Thud raised his head with a kind of scientific inspiration, for a new theory had entered his brain.

"Champer," said he to the porter, "how was the keeper cured who, as you told me, was bitten here by a snake?"

"He had ammonia rubbed in, and had ammonia mixed with water poured down his throat," was Champer's reply.

"And he recovered?" asked Thud.

"Yes, he recovered," replied the man with a grin; "but the snake warn't a poisonous un."

"Still, it's clear that ammonia is the antidote to a serpent's poison."

"Maybe it is, maybe it ain't," said the man.

"And no one can deny," pursued Thud, "that with every evil under the sun the wise thing is to go to the fountain-head, the source."

"The fountain-head, the source," echoed Champer,

without the slightest comprehension of what the oracle meant.

"Now, what is the source, the fountain-head of a serpent's poison. Is it not the serpent's fang?" cried Thud.

"Certainly, the serpent's fang," said the echo.

"Then my theory is, that if ammonia corrects poison in the blood of a bitten man, it would be far more effectual, and economical too, to introduce it, not into the wound, but into the jaws that might inflict such a wound. Is not this self-evident?" asked the philosopher, appealing to Champer.

"Self-evident," repeated the echo, but with a very faint comprehension of the orator's logic.

"You grant this," said Thud. "Then the sure way to prevent deaths from snake-bites would be to pour ammonia on the fangs of the snakes."

"If you could catch 'em," suggested old Champer.

"We have four snakes in the case," continued Thud. "No, I remember that two died yesterday; but we have the cobra still. From this little glass-stoppered bottle of ammonia I mean to pour some drops into his mouth, and so render his poison innocuous for ever."

"If the cobra don't object," observed Champer, grinning again.

"Here's the case with its strong wire-work covering," said Thud. "I am going to prove the truth of my theory."

Feeling like a second Jenner, Thucydides Thorn advanced to the case. The cobra looked sleepy, and averse to experiments being tried upon him. He would not be stirred up, even when Thud poked him with a straw introduced between the wires. The sulky snake would not open his jaws.

Thud dropped a little ammonia from the bottle through the wire cover; it fell on the cobra's head and on one of its glittering eyes. The reptile was thoroughly roused, swelled out his hood, and twisted about in angry contortions.

"I have not managed to get the ammonia on his fangs yet," cried Thud; "but he's opening his jaws wide enough now."

The young experimentalist, holding the bottle ready, and eagerly watching for an opportunity, bent over the cage. The reptile evidently saw him, for the cobra darted out his forked tongue, and seemed ready to spring; but Thud felt no fear, for he knew that strong wire-work effectually imprisoned the serpent. But whilst the philosopher held the bottle in his right hand, he unconsciously let the left press heavily on the wires, which were not so close as to prevent a small portion of a finger being exposed to the enemy's attack. There was a spring from below, a cry from above.

"Oh, I am bitten!" cried Thud, staggering back from the cage and dropping the bottle.

"Then you are a dead man!" ejaculated Champer.

The prognostication was too soon fulfilled : poor Thud had received his mortal wound, and expired within half-an-hour of receiving the bite. His end was in character with his career. There was no epitaph over Thud's grave, or it might have run thus : " Here lies Thucydides Thorn, a victim to his own theories, a martyr to science, of which he spoke so much and comprehended so little."

CHAPTER XXVIII.

UNWILLING WITNESSES.

THE confession of Oscar Coldstream received in London, and published in all the papers, did indeed excite a great deal of interest in England. It was the subject of articles in religious periodicals, was commented on from pulpits, and was looked upon as an unprecedented instance of the power of conscience.*

Nowhere was greater excitement caused than in a small sitting-room in a second-class lodging-house in Dover, where two elderly ladies were sitting together, one engaged in knitting. Miss Deborah was reading aloud to Miss Betsy a newspaper lent to them by a neighbour, for the sisters did not indulge in the luxury of taking one in for themselves. Suddenly Deborah stopped short, and her mittened hands shook so violently that she almost dropped the newspaper.

"What is the matter, Deborah?" asked her sister in alarm. "You look as if you had seen a ghost!"

---

* If unprecedented then, not a solitary instance now, as Constance Kent voluntarily confessed herself guilty of murder, and was sentenced to imprisonment for life in the present reign.

"Oh, it is all out—the murder is out! The wretched man has confessed that it was he who threw poor young Manly down the cliff on that terrible, terrible day!"

Betsy was usually slow and sedate, but she now almost snatched the paper from Deborah's hand, that her eyes might confirm the witness of her ears. She read the paragraph headed *A Murderer's Confession* with tears running down her cheeks.

To explain the cause of such strong emotion, we must recur to what had happened more than a year before.

The reader may have inferred from silence on the subject that there had been no witnesses of Walter's fatal fall. Such, however, had not been the case. It is true that Manly had purposely chosen for his difficult and dangerous ascent a time when Dover was attracted by the "new and astounding exhibition" of a conjurer who was going his rounds. Walter felt that the presence of spectators would affect his chance of winning his foolish bet—a shout of encouragement or a cry of alarm from below might make him lose his foothold. But not every one cared for the conjurer's exhibition, and the Misses Demster could not easily spare their shillings to see it, so they took an evening stroll on the beach instead. They were the daughters of a deceased clergyman; highly respectable ladies with moderate means, who tried to eke out a slender patrimony by letting out furnished lodgings in the season, and occupying them themselves when visitors were few. The Misses

Demster were specimens of a pretty numerous class of reduced gentlewomen, whom poverty does not rob of a claim to respect. Both were of kindly nature and pious character, and they were strongly attached to each other. Miss Deborah looked on her elder sister as a model of perfection. Deborah could not claim such merit for herself; she had the care of the housekeeping, and housekeeping on slender means is often a trial to temper. The good lady knew that she was often angry with the butcher, and impatient with Lizzie, the dull-witted maid-of-all-work. Miss Betsy, who was not exposed to such daily temptation, and who was brought little in contact with any one but a sister who deemed her an oracle of wisdom and a model of virtue, was rather disposed to accept Deborah's opinion as a correct one. Miss Betsy never put the thought into words, was scarcely sensible that she harboured it, but her real estimate of herself was not much unlike that of the Pharisee in the parable: "Lord, I thank Thee that we are not as other women are. We, on our narrow means, never run into debt, but give to charities a tithe of all we possess. We go to church daily, fair weather or foul, and teach in a Sunday school. We pay wages and bills with regularity; we harm no one, and are useful to many." Miss Demster set up her own standard of perfection, and was honestly convinced that she had nearly if not quite attained thereto. She taught Sunday scholars that our duty is to love God with all

our heart, soul, and strength, and our neighbour as ourselves; but it never occurred to Betsy to test her own
character by a standard so high, so divine.

The two ladies were taking their walk beneath the
cliffs on that evening when Manly was attempting his
perilous feat. Deborah saw him climbing, and tightly
grasped the arm of her sister.

"O Betsy! Betsy! look! look! that must be that
hare-brained Walter Manly, who won the steeple-chase,
attempting to climb to the top! Oh, mercy! I cannot
bear to see him; he will fall, and be dashed to pieces!"

Miss Demster, with equal interest, watched the young
man's ascent.

"He'll never do it," exclaimed Deborah. "See what
a place he has reached; he will never get up that.
What fools these boys are to risk precious life for
nothing!"

"He's a wonderful climber!" cried Betsy, as she
breathlessly watched efforts which seemed to her almost
superhuman.

"He's nearly at the top now; he's stopping to take
breath; he dare not look down or he's lost!" exclaimed
Deborah in nervous excitement. "There—there—he
has one hand on the top of the cliff!"

"Now the other; he will swing himself up!" cried
Betsy. But even as the words were on her lips her look
of interest changed to one of intense horror, and the
next moment poor Walter fell, turning over head fore-

most in the terrible fall. The once fine powerful climber lay a corpse with a broken neck at the foot of the cliff.

The two ladies hastened to the spot, overwhelmed with horror and distress.

"Dead, quite dead!" exclaimed Deborah in much sorrow. "We cannot carry the poor corpse ourselves; we must hasten off for assistance."

"Stop! stop!" gasped Miss Demster, shaking as if in a violent fit of ague. "You saw it as well as I. He did not slip; he was flung down. Oh, mercy! he was *murdered!* I saw the wretch who did the deed."

"I saw some one too," cried Deborah.

"I shall never forget the murderer's face—the handsomest face that ever I saw in my life, but fierce as a demon's. I could swear to it in a court of justice," said Betsy.

"Oh, don't talk of swearing or of courts of justice," exclaimed the younger sister nervously; "it would be too dreadful to think of."

"Of course there will be an inquest," said Miss Demster. "We shall be called as witnesses."

"I would not go for the world!" cried Deborah. "Besides, if we took an oath to tell *all* the truth, we should have to speak of the murder."

Betsy's thin lips turned white as she faltered out, "We might get a man *hanged!*"

"Oh, horrible! horrible!" exclaimed poor Deborah; "I would almost rather be hanged myself."

"We had better hurry away then, and leave some one else to find the body—some one who would not be mixed up in a murder case, as we should be certain to be." Seizing her sister by the arm, Miss Demster almost dragged her away from the spot.

But the ladies had not gone far before they both stopped as by a common impulse. "Are we doing right?" came almost simultaneously from the lips of both.

"Suppose that through us a murderer escape?" said Miss Demster. "If he commit another murder, shall we be quite clear of the guilt of the crime?"

"Or the murder may be discovered, but not the right person, and an innocent man be hanged." Deborah's terrible suggestion made both the ladies shudder.

"I tell you what we'll do," said Miss Demster, after some minutes of painful reflection: "we'll hurry home and say nothing about the matter, unless some innocent poor man be seized, and then we'll come forward and declare all that we saw, and give evidence that it was a gentleman—I mean, one who looked like a gentleman—who committed the murder."

This was a compromise with conscience, and any compromise with conscience is a dangerous thing. However, for the time it half quieted the minds of the two poor ladies.

They hurried home, hardly heeding the furious blast which suddenly rose, and which, had they been at the top of the cliffs, would almost have blown them off their feet. Miss Demster opened the door of her house with a trembling hand. There was a kind of hope in her mind that once within the quiet little dwelling trouble, like the stormy wind, could be shut out; but memory and consciousness of having evaded a duty could not be excluded. Hard did the sisters try to persuade themselves that they had only done what was natural and right. Betsy thought of the history of Achan, and recalled other instances in Scripture of sin being brought to light. Deborah remembered stories of murder having been found out when there had seemed to be no clue by which to discover who had committed the crime.

A neighbour dropped in just when the ladies were attempting to eat their frugal supper, for which all appetite was gone. The storm by this time had lulled.

" O Miss Demster, Miss Deborah, have you heard the shocking, shocking news?" cried the visitor, throwing herself down on a seat. "Poor young Manly has been found, with his neck and ever so many other bones broken, at the bottom of a cliff!"

" Indeed!" exclaimed the sisters, their consciences pricking them sorely for expressing such hypocritical surprise.

" He had evidently fallen when attempting an impossible feat. You were intending to take a walk in that direction, I know. Did you hear nothing, see nothing, of this dreadful accident?"

Miss Demster **actually** knocked over the tea-tray, smashed her cherished china, and **sent** the boiling contents of the pot over the carpet and her visitor's feet. It was her desperate resource for avoiding giving a reply.

The doctoring of the scalded feet, the picking up of the broken fragments of china, did divert attention from the subject of poor Walter. Betsy made many excuses for awkwardness—she who was never awkward; Deborah ran for cotton-wool to put over the scald; the visitor presently departed limping (her house was but two doors off), and the Demsters had kept their terrible secret.

"Deborah, we can't stand this kind of thing!" exclaimed Betsy, as soon as the outer door was shut. "Manly's fall will be the talk of all Dover, and I can't break cups and saucers every time that an uncomfortable question is asked. We'll be off to London by the stage-coach to-morrow."

And off the Demsters did go, though at great inconvenience. They could ill afford the serious expense, and a journey in February gave severe colds to both the sisters. They did not return till the nine days' wonder was over; and a coroner's inquest having been held on the body of Walter, a verdict had been given—" Accidental death by a fall from a cliff."

It is a true saying that a little sin troubles more than a great deal of sorrow, and its truth was proved by the amiable ladies in Paradise Square. The quiet, even tenor of their lives was destroyed; they felt almost like hypocrites when they taught Sunday scholars to be straightforward and truthful; they took no pleasure in going to church; they were half afraid to partake of Holy Communion.

" And yet what would every one say if we turned away ? " cried Betsy.

" Oh, how wretched we should feel!" sighed Deborah. " Oh that we had had the courage to do what was right! And yet I am afraid, should all happen over again, that I should never dare to give evidence that might cause a man to be hanged."

A thorn in the flesh often brings a man nearer to God; a thorn in the conscience severs from communion with God. The former may be endured with patience; the latter must be drawn out, or the wound rankles and festers.

The reader will now understand the emotion with which the Misses Demster read of Oscar Coldstream's confession.

" That poor sinner has some good in him," observed the elder—" he has had the courage to speak the whole truth. Perhaps he acted under great provocation, and repented of the deed as soon as it was done."

" He has done all he can to redeem the past," said Deborah, wiping her eyes. " I wonder what will be done with the poor gentleman. They will hardly hang him for telling the truth."

"You see that a commission is coming to Dover to inquire into the matter," observed Miss Demster, pointing to the end of the paragraph. "Deborah, Deborah, ought we not even now to make clean breasts, and confess all that we know?"

"That was just what I was thinking," replied poor Deborah. "We have had no peace since we hid that dreadful matter, and now our speaking out will not cause any one to be hanged."

"That Mr. Coldstream—whatever else he may be—is a brave and conscientious man," observed Betsy. "I think—though it would be an effort, a horrible effort—that we ought to give evidence now."

And the poor ladies did appear in court, their heads bowed down with shame, and veils over their faces. They received meekly and with much self-abasement the reproof of the eminent lawyer appointed to examine into the case.

"Ladies, you may hitherto have suppressed facts, and tried to defeat justice, from motives of humanity," said he; "but know that he who conceals another's crime becomes an accessory after the deed; he who shields a murderer from justice may be regarded as being, in some measure, a partaker in his guilt."

It was a consolation to the poor Misses Demster that Oscar Coldstream was not to be hanged after all. His

crime had been unpremeditated and voluntarily confessed ; he was therefore recommended to mercy. In-
structions were forwarded to the Indian Government that
the murderer of Walter Manly should be transported to
the nearest penal settlement, to remain there for the
term of his natural life.

CHAPTER XXIX.

THE SENTENCE.

BANISHMENT for life to the Andaman Islands—to the place which the natives of India speak of as "beyond the black waters," a kind of Stygian pit into which the foul drains of guilt, the slimy streams of vice throughout Hindostan, empty themselves; where there is the society of murderers and thieves; a place of mysterious misery, like the fabled infernal regions;—to Oscar Coldstream this was a sentence more terrible even than that of public execution. Such banishment was a kind of living death which, to one not yet thirty years of age, might endure for forty years or more! What frightful consequences had been entailed on Oscar by half a minute's yielding to passion! When he received the final sentence, Coldstream realized to the full extent what earthly misery he had brought on himself.

By the same ship which carried the decision regarding Oscar's fate, came also a letter from his sister-in-law, Jane Thorn, addressed to himself. Jane deplored Oscar's miserable condition; but earnestly, solemnly implored him not to let his innocent wife share in his exile. The home which was about to be Jane's should always, she wrote, be shared by her dearly-loved sister. Let Io return to England and try to forget the past.

"Yes, let her forget me—the unworthy, the guilty! Why should her young life be blighted? I do not wish to be remembered in my living grave!" And with the brief comment, "You had better do what your sister desires," Oscar handed the open letter to Io.

Her eyes streaming with tears, her hands clasped round the neck of her husband, Io replied in the words of Ruth, "Entreat me not to leave thee, nor to depart from following after thee; for where thou goest, I *will* go; and where thou diest, I will die." The last word was lost in a sob.

"But, my beloved, you have not permission to go with—a convict," said Oscar, scarcely able to command his voice.

"I will have it! I will have it!" cried Io.

The door of the cell opened; the jailer was bringing in the prisoner's meal. Io availed herself of the opportunity of quitting the place in which she had been locked up with her husband. Repeating, "I will have it; I will not return without it," she ran—she almost flew—down the long corridor, like a bird escaping from a snare. Until the rebound came, Io had scarcely realized how heavy had been the pressure of a weight on her heart—the fear, the secret dread that Oscar's might be a capital sentence. Relieved from that weight, the poor wife's spirit rebounded almost into joy. " He is safe—his precious, precious life is safe!" Io kept repeating to herself, as she quitted the dark, dismal prison. " The Lord can make him happy yet; and as for me, it is happiness to be with him."

Io did not find the palanquin at the entrance, for no one had expected her to quit the prison so soon. She stopped the first empty conveyance which she saw. " To Government House " was the direction which she gave to the driver. She had entered that lordly building but once before—on her arrival as a bride at Calcutta. Io had gone in goodly apparel, and her beauty had attracted much admiration. " Coldstream has drawn a prize," had been the Governor-General's remark to a friend. How changed was all now! And yet Io was fairer in the dark weeds which she wore for her mother, nobler in the devotion which she showed to a husband ruined and disgraced, than she had been at her presentation at a semi-regal court.

On her arrival at the stately palace in which the ruler of India resided, Io found that her humble vehicle could not be driven up to the handsome entrance. Before the pillared portico stood a splendid carriage drawn by tall camels with trappings of scarlet and gold, preceded by outriders on gaily-caparisoned steeds. The Governor-General was going out to attend a review.

" I am just in time," thought Io, as she threw open

the door of her conveyance and sprang out. Through the little crowd of gaping Orientals waiting to see the Lord Sahib "eat the air," past outriders, and all the glittering paraphernalia of princely state, glided Io Coldstream, too intent on her errand to heed anything around her.

The Governor-General was at the top of the flight of broad steps, which he was about to descend, conversing with one of the *aides-de-camp* who were in attendance on the great man. Io rapidly mounted the steps, all gazing at her, but no one hindering. She fell at the Governor-General's feet, clasped her hands, and in a voice of passionate entreaty exclaimed, "Oh, grant me leave to share my husband's exile!"

"Mrs. Coldstream! my dear lady!" exclaimed the Governor-General, raising the suppliant, whom he had at once recognized, "is it possible that you can wish to go to the settlement, where all the surroundings will be so utterly uncongenial?"

"I care not for surroundings; I have but one desire, one favour to implore—to be allowed to go with my husband. You cannot, you will not, refuse that one little boon!" cried Io.

"Madam, I honour your devotion; I sympathize with your sorrows; I cannot refuse your petition," said the Governor, visibly affected.

Mrs. Coldstream was not suffered to depart in the humble vehicle in which she had come, gladly as she would have escaped from the uncongenial glare and glitter; for, now that her petition was granted, Io realized her position as the wife of a felon. A handsome carriage was placed at her disposal, and the highest officer in the Governor-General's suite would have been proud to act as her escort. Io was impatient of delay, for the vessel which was to bear its sad cargo of criminals to the place of punishment was to sail in two days. There were preparations to be made for the voyage and the life-long exile. Io very gratefully thanked the Governor-General for all his kindness; but it was with a sigh of relief that she found herself at last on the way to the missionary's house in which, through all the long months of suspense and waiting, she had found a quiet home.

The missionary's wife received her guest in the veranda. Mrs. Leveson, like the rest of the Calcutta world, had heard of Mr. Coldstream's sentence. She took the weary young wife into her motherly arms.

"Oh, dear Mrs. Leveson, I have so much, so very much to do and to think of!" cried Io. "I so need to have the quiet waiting spirit of a Mary, but I must do the work of a Martha. I have so much purchasing and packing before me, that I shall hardly have time to-morrow even to go to my husband."

"I will do the purchasing and packing, dear child," said the kind-hearted lady. "You have nothing to do but to give me a list of what you require."

Very thankfully was this kindness accepted. Io would scarcely wait to throw off her bonnet, tired and heated as she was, before sitting down to draw up her list of requirements. As she was completing it, Mrs. Leveson glanced over her shoulder. " My dear child, ' a *colour-box* and a supply of *cardboard!* ' " she read out in a tone of surprise.

" Yes, my Oscar paints beautifully ; he will need every resource. I am taking his flute also. Alas ! he has not touched it since our marriage ! "

" And you have forgotten a waterproof cloak for yourself when going to a place noted for dampness," said Mrs. Leveson. " Dear Mrs. Coldstream, I shall have to revise your list, as well as to execute your commissions."

CHAPTER XXX.

CONSOLATION.

As soon as Io quitted the prison cell of her husband, Oscar gave vent to the anguish which he had hardly been able to restrain in her presence. Leaving the loathed food untouched, the unhappy criminal paced up and down the narrow space in which he was confined, with hands tightly clasped and raised towards heaven with a gesture of something like despair.

"The brand of Cain is upon me!" he groaned; "and like Cain, I am driven forth a vagabond on the earth. Like him, I cry, 'My punishment is greater than I can bear!' Is it sinful to pray that this misery may not be a prolonged one? Is it sinful to implore to be soon released from the worse than Egyptian bondage to which my mad wickedness has brought me, and to which I am dragging down with me my sweet, innocent wife?"

The unexpected sound of footsteps in the corridor, then that of the key grating in the lock of his cell, startled the prisoner, for no one usually came at that hour. The heavy, nail-studded door slowly unclosed, the jailer entered **to introduce a visitor,** and then him-self retired.

" Lawrence!"—"**My** friend!" **The brief** greetings were exchanged, **and the** chaplain **and** the prisoner em-braced, as brothers might embrace **who were never** again to meet **in this world.**

For some minutes no other **word was spoken. Oscar** was the first to break **the** silence.

" How came you **to see me here—in my prison ?"** he asked.

"I could stay away no longer," **was the** chaplain's reply. ."I felt that I must see my friend **once more."**

" You call me *friend,*" said **Oscar gloomily.**

" Friend—yes, brother!" cried Lawrence.

" You forget *why* **I am here,"** said the criminal.

" No, I do not forget that you are here because you had the courage to confess **your deed;** because you preferred punishment **and** disgrace to honour and ease ; because *you dared to pluck* **out the right** *eye.* Cold-stream, do you repent having made a confession ?"

" Never!" was the emphatic reply. **"I would** rather suffer any earthly misery **than** the terrible separation from God which I **once had to** endure."

" Then indeed you are **my** brother in Christ," said the chaplain. " Are we **not both sinners** redeemed by grace ?"

Lawrence's coming **was to** Oscar as a draught **of** cool **and** sweet refreshing water to one perishing of thirst.

The friends sat down together, and long was the conversation which ensued. Coldstream spoke more freely to Lawrence of his grief than he had done to Io, for he was less afraid of inflicting pain. Lawrence gave heart-felt sympathy, and he gave consolation besides. The chaplain spoke of the tears of a David and the penitence of a Peter. He touched on the story of the woman deeply sunken in sin, who was offered freely the water of life by Him who was to die to procure it. Was not that woman to become a missionary to her own people? Was not David to prepare for the building of the Temple? Was not Peter to live an apostle and die a martyr?

"God may have some work for you to do even in the place of your exile," said Lawrence. "The Lord asks not, 'Hast thou ever sinned greatly against Me?' but He says, 'Lovest thou Me?' You can give the same answer as did the penitent Peter."

"I can, I can," murmured Coldstream under his breath.

"Then, though severed from country and friends, you have a Home and a Father on high."

After a few minutes of silent thought, Oscar said, in a hesitating tone, "Do you think that it would be sinful presumption in me to partake once more of the Supper of the Lord?"

"One of my chief objects in coming to Calcutta was to see if you could receive from me Holy Communion," said Mark.

" It would be a great comfort, a great privilege," said Coldstream ; " one from which sin has for long shut me out."

The prison authorities put no difficulties in the way ; they had from the first treated their unhappy charge with consideration. On the following morning the dreary cell became, as it were, a chapel. Over the rude table, on which former criminals had carved their names, a spotless white cloth was spread, covering every mark and unsightly stain. Before it knelt Oscar and his wife, with their missionary friends. It was a holy, peaceful service. Oscar felt that there was a blessing even for a sinner such as he. *Blessed is he whose transgression is pardoned, and whose sin is covered ; blessed is the man to whom the Lord imputeth not sin.*

CHAPTER XXXI.

THE VOYAGE.

AWAY, away over the wide waters; farewell, a long, a last farewell to the civilized world! Coldstream's parting with Lawrence is over; both felt that they should never look on each other's face on this side the grave, but that they should meet on the other side. The breeze fills out the swelling sails; the vessel bounds over the waves. The smell of the sea, the glitter on the waters, the sense of having only the blue sky above, exercised a sensible influence on both the Coldstreams. A slight tinge of colour came to Oscar's pale, thin cheeks, and Io's dark eyes brightened with something like pleasure.

"It is nice to be again on the free billows," she said; and she mentally added, "These so-called black waters are wondrously blue."

There were other convicts on board besides Coldstream, but with most of them no communication could be held, such a diversity of tongues is found in the vast extent of India. There were, however, one Burmese man, and a woman who was a Bengali. Some knowledge of the language of the latter Io had picked up during her weary stay in Calcutta.

The Burmese looked with curiosity on the fair, youthful lady, bound, like himself, to the Andaman Islands. Oscar heard the man muttering to himself, " I wonder what bad thing *she* has done? She doesn't look like one of our sort."

" The lady has done nothing bad," said Coldstream ; " she only goes into exile because she will not desert her husband."

" My boy's mother is not like that," observed the Burmese with a gloomy smile; " she would never go across the black waters for me, though it was through her that I got into all this trouble."

" What did you do ? " asked Oscar, who saw that the manly-looking fellow seemed inclined for conversation.

" A rascally Mussulman pulled off the veil of my boy's mother. I was not going to stand that, so I stuck my knife into him. But he did not die," added the Burmese.

" Are you not glad that he did not die ? " asked Oscar.

" Not I," was the fierce reply. " I would as soon be hanged as sent across the black waters. If the thing came over again, I'd do just the same as I did."

Io, in the meantime, had gone up to the Bengali woman, who, in her soiled *sari*, was crouching on the deck in an attitude of hopeless dejection.

Io made the most of her little stock of Bengali ; her

gentle, winning manner **went** further than her words. She at length **made the** convict look **up, and, after a considerable time, drew** from her something **like the** following tale :—

"**The** children's father* **did not** love me. **He** wanted a boy, and only girls came—one, two, three, *four* girls ! The last was very **little; I could carry** her **in my** hand —like that. **I could give her** no nourishment; baby was thin—you could count all **her** bones. She cried all day and **all night.** Baby's **father was** angry at **the** crying; he said **he would** throw her into the Ganges. So I put **her under water;** and a sahib saw it, and gave me into the charge **of** the sepoys. **If** I **had put a** little poison **into baby's** mouth, no one would **have** known anything about **it.**"

"How horrible !" exclaimed Io, intuitively drawing back. "How could you hurt your **own baby ?**"

"**I** did not hurt her; **I put her to** rest," said the woman, who was utterly unconscious **of** having committed a **sin.**

Io went and compared **notes** with her husband, **who** had had a long talk with the Burmese convict.

"Neither of these **poor** creatures has any sense **of** the heinousness of their guilt," observed Oscar. "The man acted from an idea **of** honour; the woman thought **it** no cruelty to still **the** wailings **of a** miserable, unwelcomed babe."

* It would be deemed very improper for a woman to say "my husband."

"O Oscar, if these be specimens of our future companions in banishment, you have a grand, a glorious work before you!"

The same thought had flashed across the mind of Coldstream. Was it not possible that the Lord was indeed guiding by His eye one unworthy of the least of all His mercies, and guiding to a position of greater usefulness than Coldstream had ever occupied before?

The Coldstreams, during the rest of the voyage, devoted much time to teaching their convict companions, and, both with Burmese and Bengali, the seed of the Word appeared to fall into ground softened by sorrow. Poor Lachmi, who had been down-trodden by man, and terrified by legends regarding demon-like deities, clung to the thought that there was one religion of love. The Burmese received the truth in simplicity, and rejoiced to hear that there was One who would stand his Friend, though the world had cast him off. Nor was this all. Coldstream found ready listeners in the Lascars who manned the vessel, and who had never before had any one to speak to them of a Saviour. The captain, a rough, honest Englishman, watched with surprise the quiet but earnest work which was turning his ship into a floating Bethel.

"I don't know how such as you ever found your way into a penal settlement," observed Captain Partridge to Coldstream on the evening before they landed. "I think I've a Jonah on board."

"One brought from lower depths than ever was Jonah," was Oscar's reply.

"And going to preach to worse sinners than those of old Nineveh," said the captain. "I see that you've brought your gourd with you," he added, as he glanced at Io, who was standing gazing in the direction of the land from which "the spicy breezes" were already wafted over the ocean.

"God grant that I may not love her too well or lose her too early," thought Coldstream; "she is all that is left to me upon earth."

CHAPTER XXXII.

"O Oscar! this can be no penal settlement; it is a paradise, a perfect paradise of beauty!" was Io's delighted exclamation as, aided by her husband, she stepped on shore. Imagination had pictured the Andamans as some hot waste of sand, or some burning rock, fit abode for criminals driven forth from their fellow-men; but perhaps the whole earth holds no fairer spot, none more favoured by nature, than these beautiful Eastern islands —"emeralds set in the ring of the sea." There plants grow in the richest luxuriance; there verdure clothes the forest, and flowers spangle the earth. Where the green waves gently lap the shore, corals of marvellous beauty may be seen through the transparent depths. Well worthy of artist's pencil or poet's lay are the dreaded Andaman Isles.

Oscar, rapt in admiration, gazed on the scene around him.

"Strange — most wonderful!" burst from his lips. "Adam was for one sin banished from paradise, and my sin, far more detestable than his, has brought me into another Eden."

"Not your sin, beloved one, say not your sin!" exclaimed Io; "rather your repentance, the brave sacrifice which you made in indeed plucking out the right eye."

"And what gave me courage to make the sacrifice?" asked Oscar, looking gratefully at his wife. "Was it not my Io's brave words when, at the crisis of my life, she said, 'Do what you think is right'?"

The Andaman Islands are governed in a humane and liberal spirit. There is no dungeon there—no chains, unless it be in Viper's Island, to which only the most desperate ruffians are transported to be kept under stricter ward. The chief commissioner has indeed the power of life or death, and soldiers to carry his orders into effect; but when the Coldstreams arrived they found themselves under the sway of a wise and beneficent ruler. The commissioner received Oscar with grave politeness, his wife with chivalrous courtesy.

"I am afraid, Mr. Coldstream," said the commissioner, "that I must make no exception in your favour. Our people here have small allotments of land, and are expected to cultivate them with their own hands."

"I wish for no exception in my favour, sir," was the convict's reply; "I deserve none, for there is no one in these islands who has sinned so grievously against the laws of God and man as myself."

To Oscar Coldstream his manual labour became a pleasure. No land was better cultivated than his; and he made his hut a bower of beauty, in which the bird of paradise was Io.

But the principal labour of both the Coldstreams was amongst the convicts of either sex. The English couple were earnest missionaries without the name. Year by year souls were won for the Master, and out of the chaos of misery and crime a little church of lowly believers gradually rose. Oscar had no children. This was to him not a matter of regret, for he could not have endured to leave to his offspring a heritage of disgrace, the name of the sons of a felon. But the Coldstreams were granted many spiritual children, and the ties formed in the Andaman Islands were to Oscar and Io so close and so dear, that even had a pardon come they would have declined leaving their place of exile, or rather their sphere of work. Oscar was known amongst the people as the *pir*, or saint—a title which he always repudiated, but which clung to him still.

Letters connected the Coldstreams with the outer world, and not unfrequently the chief commissioner lent newspapers to read. Oscar knew when a fair young queen ascended the throne which this worthy descendant of Alfred still fills. He received from Mark Lawrence the glad news that after years of loneliness his home was to be brightened by the presence of a wife. The chaplain's former disappointment had been in itself a blessing, for without it he would have been linked to one who would not have made him happy.

With one scene in the life of the Coldstreams, about eight years after their arrival in the Andaman Islands, my little story concludes.

"There is a vessel in the offing, my Oscar," said Io one morning; "shall we go down and see the arrivals?"

Oscar was just putting the last touches to a beautiful water-colour picture which was to be a birthday present to Io; but he rose at once, put down his brush, and prepared to accompany his wife.

"Formerly," observed Oscar, "it was with sadness that we saw new-comers arriving; now hope counterbalances pity. We look upon prisoners coming to the Andaman Islands less as sinners to be punished than as souls that may be saved."

"But these are not prisoners; they come in the commissioner's yacht. There are nice white English faces," exclaimed Io joyfully, quickening her pace, "and one is a lady! O Oscar, Oscar!" she continued in the excitement of pleasure, "I am certain that yonder is Mark Lawrence, and she who leans on his arm must be his wife!"

Oscar hurried on so fast at the word that Io had to run to keep up with his pace. Here was a great and unexpected pleasure indeed! In a few minutes the friends who had deemed that they were parted for ever as regards this world were greeting each other with cordial delight.

"You never thought—I never thought of my being appointed chaplain to the troops in the Andaman Islands!" cried Mark, after having with pleasure and pride introduced his young wife. "Why, Coldstream, the climate of the place must suit you, for you look little changed after so many years of residence, only more strong and a little more sunburnt." Lawrence might have added, "and a great deal more happy," for Coldstream's fine countenance now wore an expression of peace.

And Io was blooming still, not a silver thread in the auburn hair, not a wrinkle of care on the white smooth brow. The water-lily had again opened its chalice to the sunshine, and was smiling in the light which came from heaven, and was reflected by very many objects around her.

That day was one of the happiest which the Coldstreams had ever known. No stranger seeing the group that sat eagerly chatting over old days would have dreamed that the one gentleman was a chaplain, the other a convict. Oscar himself was the only one to whose mind came the recollection of his great crime; in his heart of hearts was written, "Jesus Christ came to save sinners, *of whom I am chief.*"

A party to visit a spot of singular beauty was arranged for a later hour of the day. The distance was so short that in the evening even the ladies could walk.

"I have a double object in selecting Palm-tree Point," observed Coldstream: "I have just received notice that a Karen is lying in a hut there with a broken leg. I have not seen him yet, for he is a recent arrival."

"I could almost wish that it were our old friend Ko Thah Byu," said Lawrence.

"One would hardly find him *here*," rejoined Cold-stream.

In the softened light of a rich sunset the Lawrences and Coldstreams made their way to the beautiful spot. They found the Karen, not in the hut, but stretched on a *charpai* under a tree. None of the visitors had ever seen the man before, but the fact of his being a Karen awakened additional interest.

After kindly salutation, and making inquiries after the injury which the convict had received, Coldstream, taking a seat on a mat, opened his Karen Bible. The ladies rested themselves luxuriously on a mossy bank garlanded with rare ferns.

"Ah, that is the book which Ko Thah Byu so loved!" observed the Karen.

"Did you know him?" asked Oscar.

"I knew him well," said the sufferer. "Ko Thah Byu often came to our village to give the good tidings of great joy. If I had minded all that he said I should never have come to this place."

"I must try to find out where he is," observed Lawrence, "and give him news of you."

The convict shook his head sadly. "Ko Thah Byu is where news cannot reach him," said the Karen. "Our brother has gone to be with the Lord. I was at his side when he died."

The tidings were received with sorrow. How apt are we to grudge the victor his crown, the weary labourer his rest! We grieve to think that a familiar voice shall never again on earth proclaim God's truth, though we believe that it is swelling the chorus of His praise in heaven.

Inquiries elicited a few particulars of the last days of the first Karen convert and apostle. Ko Thah Byu had latterly been afflicted with painful sickness, and blindness had quenched the light of his piercing eyes. The evangelist had had to close his long itinerancies, and wander no more amongst the heathen. Yet as long as Ko Thah Byu could preach, he preached, bearing fruit even in old age. Then, as a ripe sheaf meet for the Master's garner, the saint fell asleep amongst his own people, honoured, beloved, and lamented.

" Of the Karen apostle it may well be said," observed the chaplain, " that he will have many stars in his crown."

" May I, unworthy as I am, be reckoned amongst them !" said Oscar Coldstream with emotion. " I should, humanly speaking, never have known peace on earth or glory in heaven had I not been taught by the Karen the force of the inspired words: *Blessed is he whose transgression is forgiven, whose sin is covered......I acknowledged my sin unto Thee, and mine iniquity have I not hid. I said, I will confess my transgressions unto the Lord; and Thou forgavest the iniquity of my sin.*"

APPENDIX.

WHILST some readers will skip the appendix altogether, to others it may appear the best part of my book, as it will give some information regarding the present state of the Karens, and will show what sorts of fruit now grow on the tree planted by the devoted American missionaries and their first convert, Ko Thah Byu.

I will not dwell long on the fact mentioned in secular newspapers, that when the English took possession of Burmah those of the inhabitants *trusted with arms* were loyal Karens, as they would defend the laws. Such courage was displayed by the Karens that they were given by the English Government a large reward.

It is more interesting to know how the Christian Karens have honoured the memory of their apostle, Ko Thah Byu. I will give some extracts from his memoir, to which I have been already indebted:—

"On the 16th of this month, May 1878, occurred the fiftieth anniversary of the baptism of the first Karen convert, Ko Thah Byu. He was not only the first in time. As a humble, persistent, and prayerful teacher of the gospel to his heathen countrymen, he ranks easily first amongst the hundreds of faithful men who have succeeded him."

A school and building fund was raised, not only with a view to usefulness in the growing church, but to erect a worthy monument to Ko Thah Byu. To give another extract :—

"It was voted, in view of the exigency and the jubilee, to make a special thank-offering, that the missionary hall might be dedicated without delay. It was the hottest time of the year, but every man, woman, and child stayed at his post. An enthusiasm for giving fell on the people. On the day of dedication our new building fund, which we had set at the modest figure of 20,000 rupees (less than £2,000), reached the sum of 42,342 rupees. The debt was extinguished; there was abundance of material on hand, and over 8,000 rupees in cash......To sum up, since 1868 the Karens of Bassein alone have sent 43,050 rupees for the erection of permanent and substantial buildings."

Then follows a detailed description of the opening of the Ko Thah Byu Mission Hall, the winding up of which we will give to our readers :—

"On the wall of the south veranda we have carved in large gilded Burmese characters—

1828. Ko Thah Byu. 1878.

And our prayer is that the building may long stand, and do its part towards training and sending forth hundreds of men and women far better equipped for the service of the Master than Ko Thah Byu, and with a spirit no less fervent and devoted."

To bring the account of the Karens to a still later date, I give an extract of a comparatively recent speech made by a lady, the only Karen missionary at a large conference.* Speaking of the interesting people amongst whom she laboured, she said : " Without any literature, they had a tradition about some old book which had been taken from them, but which some day the white men would bring back to them. They were therefore ready to receive the gospel, and when it reached them they yielded readily to its power. Now there are *over 450 parishes, with their own pastors and schools.* They also send out missionaries to the regions beyond. *There are 30,000 Church communicants.* Many of the young men have gone with their wives across the hills far north amongst strange peoples, and are there preaching the gospel...... There is a Women's Karen Missionary Society."

* Held, I think, in 1888, but it may have been in the previous year.

Favourite Stories by A. L. O. E.

Exiles in Babylon ; or, Children of Light. With 34 Engravings. Crown 8vo, cloth extra, gilt edges. Price 5s.

A lively tale, in which are skilfully introduced lectures on the history of Daniel.

Hebrew Heroes. A Tale founded on Jewish History. With 28 Engravings. Crown 8vo, cloth extra, gilt edges. Price 5s.

A story founded on that stirring period of Jewish history, the wars of Judas Maccabæus. The tale is beautifully and truthfully told, and presents a faithful picture of the period and the people.

Pictures of St. Peter in an English Home. Crown 8vo, cloth extra, gilt edges. Price 5s.

"A. L. O. E. invokes the aid of entertaining dialogue, and probably may have more readers than all the other writers on St. Peter put together....The book is brilliantly written."—Presbyterian Messenger.

Rescued from Egypt. With 28 Engravings. Crown 8vo, cloth extra, gilt edges. Price 5s.

A interesting tale, toned and improved by illustrations from the history of Moses and the people of Israel.

The Shepherd of Bethlehem. With 40 Engravings. Crown 8vo, cloth extra, gilt edges. Price 5s.

A charming tale, including cottage lectures on the history of David, which the incidents of the story illustrate.

Claudia. A Tale. Post 8vo, cloth extra, gilt edges. Price 3s. 6d.

A tale for the young. Difference between intellectual and spiritual life. Pride of intellect and self-confidence humbled, and true happiness gained at last along with true humility.

Idols in the Heart. With Eight Engravings. Post 8vo, cloth extra, gilt edges. Price 3s. 6d.

A tale for the young. The story of a young wife and stepmother. Idols in the family—pride, pleasure, self-will, and too blind affection—discovered and dethroned.

The Lady of Provence ; or, Humbled and Healed. A Tale of the First French Revolution. Post 8vo, cloth extra, gilt edges. 3s. 6d.

A pious English girl made a blessing to her French mistress in the terrible scenes of the Revolution; illustrative of the Scripture story of Naaman, the Syrian general.

On the Way ; or, Places Passed by Pilgrims. With 12 Illustrations. Post 8vo, cloth extra, gilt edges. Price 3s. 6d.

A tale for the young, illustrative of a variety of incidents in Bunyan's Pilgrim.

The Spanish Cavalier. With 8 Engravings. Post 8vo, cloth extra, gilt edges. Price 3s. 6d.

A tale illustrative of modern life in Spain, and incidentally of the events of the Revolution of 1868, particularly as they relate to the recent awakening of Protestant religious feeling.

The Young Pilgrim. A Tale Illustrating the "Pilgrim's Progress." With 27 Engravings. Post 8vo, cloth extra, gilt edges. Price 3s. 6d.

A Child's Companion to the "Pilgrim's Progress." It is intended to bring the ideas of that wonderful allegory within the comprehension of the young mind.

Precepts in Practice ; or, Stories Illustrating the Proverbs. With upwards of 40 Engravings. Post 8vo, cloth extra. Price 2s.

In an attractive and entertaining way the author, in each story, makes the events of everyday life illustrate some truth taught by the wise King Solomon.

T. NELSON AND SONS, LONDON, EDINBURGH, AND NEW YORK.

Favourite Stories by A. L. O. E.

The Crown of Success; or, Four Heads to Furnish. With **Eight** Engravings. Post 8vo, cloth extra, gilt edges. Price 3s.

An allegorical tale for the young. The four cottages of Head taken and furnished by Dame Desley's four children, with the help of their friend, Mr. Learning. This book is of unusual interest to children, and very instructive. Suited for ages from ten to twelve years.

Cyril Ashley. A Tale. **Post 8vo,** cloth extra, gilt edges. **3s.**

An English tale for young persons, illustrative of some of the practical lessons to be learned from the Scripture story of Jonah the prophet.

The Giant Killer; or, The Battle which All must Fight. **Post 8vo,** cloth extra, gilt edges. **3s.**

A tale for the young, illustrating "the battle which all must fight" against the Giants Sloth, Selfishness, Untruth, Hate, and Pride.

House Beautiful; or, The Bible Museum. **Post 8vo,** cloth extra, gilt edges. **Price 3s.**

"A gallery of Scripture portraits." Short chapters on the most remarkable scenes and incidents of Scripture history. With pictorial illustrations.

The Silver Casket; or, The World and its Wiles. Illustrated. Post 8vo, cloth extra, gilt edges. 3s.

A tale for the young; partly an allegory; with scenes in the Palace of Deceits, the Forest of Temptation, etc.

War and Peace. A Tale of the Retreat from Cabul in 1842. With Eight Plates. Post 8vo, cloth extra, gilt edges. Price 3s.

This sketch of one of the saddest passages in our history has been chiefly drawn from "Lady Sale's Journal."

A Wreath of Indian Stories. Post 8vo, cloth extra, gilt edges. Price 3s.

Ten tales of native life in India; and ten short stories, illustrative of the Commandments. These stories describe, in Oriental style, the everyday scenes and customs of native life.

Battling with the World; or, The Roby Family. Illustrated. Post 8vo, cloth extra, gilt edges. Price 2s. 6d.

This tale forms a sequel to "The Giant-Killer; or, The Battle which All must Fight," by the same Author.

Flora; or, Self-Deception. Illustrated. Post 8vo, cloth extra, gilt edges. Price 2s. 6d.

The good seed springing up among stones and thorns, with too little root to bear "fruit with patience," or to withstand the force of temptation. A tale for the young.

The Haunted Room. A Tale. Post 8vo, cloth extra. 2s. 6d.

An interesting tale, intended to warn against nervous and superstitious fears and weakness, and show remedy of Christian courage and presence of mind.

The Mine; or, Darkness and Light. Illustrated. Post 8vo, cloth extra, gilt edges. 2s. 6d.

A tale for the young of a somewhat allegorical character, in which it is shown that Faith and Religion are sure guides through the most difficult paths in life. The incidents of the story are absorbing without being of a sensational character.

Miracles of Heavenly Love in Daily Life. With Eight Engravings. Post 8vo, cloth extra, gilt edges. Price 2s. 6d.

Twelve tales (some of the same characters in them all) illustrative of many of our Lord's miracles; showing that miracles of God's love, which should not be overlooked or undervalued, often occur in the common events of life.

T. NELSON AND SONS, LONDON, EDINBURGH, AND NEW YORK.

A. L. O. E.'s Books for the Young.

Edith and her Ayah, and Other Stories. With numerous Engravings. **Cloth extra. Price 1s.**

Fifteen short stories for the young.

A Friend in Need, and Other Stories. With Seven Engravings. Cloth extra. Price 1s.

Eight short tales for young readers.

Good for **Evil,** and Other Stories. With 14 Engravings. Cloth extra. Price 1s.

Nine short tales for young readers.

The **Hymn** my Mother **Taught Me,** and Other Stories. With 24 Engravings. Cloth extra. 1s.

Fourteen short tales for young readers.

The **Olive** Branch, and Other Stories. With 16 Illustrations. Cloth extra. Price 1s.

Seventeen short stories for young readers.

Try Again, and Other Stories. With numerous Engravings. Cloth extra. Price 1s.

Sixteen short tales for young readers.

Upwards and Downwards, and Other Stories. With 16 Illustrations. Cloth extra. Price 1s.

Seven short tales for young readers.

Wings and Stings. With Six Engravings. Cloth Extra. 1s.

A. L. O. E. is perhaps unequalled as a writer of allegories for children. In this volume the bees are made to afford lessons in many virtues that children should acquire. It is suitable for either boys or girls.

Stories of the Wars of the Jews. From the Babylonish Captivity to the Destruction of Jerusalem by Titus. With Coloured Frontispiece and 44 Illustrations. Cloth extra. Price 1s. 6d.

The A. L. O. E. Series.

Cloth extra. Price 6d. each.

Every Cloud has a Silver Lining.

The Backward Swing.

The Tiny Red Night-cap.

The Message **of Hope.**

Only a Little.

The Brother's Return.

The Victory.

The Truant Kitten.

Each volume of this series contains five or six pretty stories by A. L. O. E., conveying some good moral lesson.

Books by A. L. O. E.

In 1s. Packets.

Packet 1.—**The Little Sower,** and Other Stories.

1. The Little Sower.—2. Thorns and Flowers.—3. The White Robe.—4. Trusted and Trusty.

Packet 2.—**The Best Friend,** and Other Stories.

1. The Best Friend.—2. The Soldier's Child.—3. The Little Light.—4. Are all Saved?

Packet 15.—**Stories Illustrating the Proverbs.**

1. Courage and Candour.—2. A Friend in Need. &c.

Packet 18.—**Stories by A. L. O. E.**

1. Upwards and Downwards.—2. A Friend in Need.—3. The Great Plague. —4. Good for Evil. &c.

Packet 39.—**Stories by A. L. O. E. Packet A.**

1. Good-bye.—2. Don't be Too Sure.— 3. Quite in Earnest. &c.

Packet 40.—**Stories by A. L. O. E. Packet B.**

1. Bearing Burdens.—2. Grasping the Apple.—3. The Diamond Locket. &c.

T. NELSON AND SONS, LONDON, EDINBURGH, AND NEW YORK.

Library of Historical Tales.

The City and the Castle. A Story of the Reformation in Switzerland. By ANNIE LUCAS, Author of "Leonie," etc. Crown 8vo, cloth extra. Price 4s.

A tale of a noble family and one in humble life becoming connected by circumstances, the relation of which faithfully portrays the state and character of society at the time of the Reformation (in Switzerland).

Leonie; or, Light out of Darkness: and **Within Iron Walls, a** Tale of the Siege of Paris. Twin-Stories of the Franco-German War. By ANNIE LUCAS. Crown 8vo, cloth extra. Price 4s.

Two tales, the first connected with the second. One, of country life in France during the war; the other, life within the besieged capital. These stories abound in interesting and graphic sketches of French life and character, and incidentally contain a faithful description of the leading events of the Franco-German War.

Wenzel's Inheritance; or, Faithful unto Death. A Tale of Bohemia in the Fifteenth Century. By ANNIE LUCAS. Crown 8vo, cloth extra. Price 4s.

Presents a vivid picture of the religious and social condition of Bohemia in the fifteenth century. The story is one of suffering and martyrdom borne for faith's sake.

Helena's Household. A Tale of Rome in the First Century. With Frontispiece. Crown 8vo, cloth extra. Price 4s.

Illustrates the mode in which the very persecutions of the primitive ages of the Church were made instrumental, through the Spirit of God, to the promulgation of the faith.

The Spanish Brothers. A Tale of the Sixteenth Century. By the Author of "The Dark Year of Dundee." Crown 8vo, cloth extra. Price 4s.

A tale of Spanish life, presenting a true and vivid picture of the cruel and stormy time during the period of the Inquisition.

The Czar. A Tale of the Time of the First Napoleon. By the Author of "The Spanish Brothers," etc. Crown 8vo, cloth extra. Price 4s.

An interesting tale of the great Franco-Russian war in 1812–13; the characters partly French, partly Russian.

Arthur Erskine's Story. A Tale of the Days of Knox. By the Author of "The Spanish Brothers," etc. Crown 8vo, cloth extra. Price 4s.

The object of the writer of this tale is to portray the life of the people in the days of Knox. The stormy passions of the time are vividly described, and the story of Scotland's Reformation is effectively re-told.

Under the Southern Cross. A Tale of the New World. By the Author of "The Spanish Brothers," etc. Crown 8vo, cloth extra. Price 4s.

A thrilling and fascinating story, most exciting in incident, and most instructive in its accurate reproduction of the manners and customs in Peru during the later years of the sixteenth century.

Pendower. A Story of Cornwall in the Reign of Henry the Eighth. By M. FILLEUL. Crown 8vo, cloth extra. Price 4s.

A tale illustrating in fiction that stirring period of English history previous to the Reformation.

T. NELSON AND SONS, LONDON, EDINBURGH, AND NEW YORK.

Prize Temperance Tales.

Books on Bible Subjects, etc.

Illuminated Gift-Books, etc.

Thoughts for Sunrise. Daily Morning Texts and Morning Hymns. Beautifully Illuminated. Ribbon Style. Gilt edges. **1s.**

"Illuminated by L. M. W. with much taste and skill....Quite admirably produced, and printed in colours and gold." —MAGAZINE OF ART.

Thoughts for Sunset. A Book for Eventide. Beautifully Illuminated by L. M. W. Ribbon Style. Gilt edges. **Price 1s.**

"A dainty little book. The texts of Scripture are delicately illuminated by L. M. W., and the illustrative poetical selections have been judiciously gathered from a wide area."—CHRISTIAN WORLD.

Thoughts of Heaven, our Home Above. Beautifully Illuminated. Ribbon Style. Gilt edges. **1s.**

"Cannot be praised too highly for its artistic excellence."—SCOTSMAN.

For Eventide. Beautifully Illuminated with Texts and Hymns for Eight Weeks. Edited by H. L. L. Richly gilt. **Price 1s.**

"It is a little gem in its way; pleasing to the eye by its appearance, and pleasing to the heart by its contents."—FOOTSTEPS OF TRUTH.

** This Series is also kept bound in cloth extra, price 1s. 6d.; Paste grain padded, price 2s. 6d.; and in German calf, price 3s. 6d.

Glad Tidings for Pilgrims Zionward. With 12 Beautiful Illuminations and Hymns. Oblong, cloth extra, gilt edges. **1s. 6d.**

This elegant little gift book contains twelve beautiful floral cards with texts of Scripture, and on each opposite page a suitable hymn.

Eastern Manners and Customs. Selected Passages from "THE LAND AND THE BOOK." With 12 Chromo-Lithograph Illustrations. Oblong, cloth extra, gilt edges. Price 1s. **6d.**

The Feast of Sacrifice and the Feast of Remembrance; or, The Origin and Teaching of the Lord's Supper. With an Introductory Preface by the LORD BISHOP OF RIPON. Cloth, red edges. **Price 1s.**

The Evening Hymn. By the late Rev. J. D. BURNS of Hampstead. With Carmine Borders round the Pages. Royal 18mo, cloth. **1s.**

Contains a hymn and a prayer for the evenings of a month.

Within the Gates; or, Glimpses of the Heavenly Jerusalem. By the late Rev. J. D. BURNS. Carmine Borders round the Pages. Royal 18mo, cloth. **Price 1s.**

Keble's Christian Year. Thoughts in Verse for the Sundays and Holy-days throughout the Year. 18mo, red lines, cloth extra. **1s.**

Daily Bible Readings for the Lord's Household: Intended for the Family Circle or the Closet. By the late Rev. JAMES SMITH. 24mo, cloth extra, **gilt** edges. **Price 1s. 6d.**

A book for family worship or for private reading. It comprises a text followed by a short exposition and a verse of a hymn for every day in the year.

T. NELSON AND SONS, LONDON, EDINBURGH, AND NEW YORK.

Birthday and Daily Text-books.

The Bible Birthday **Book.** A Choice Selection of **Texts** for every Day in the Year. **By the Author** of "Hymns from **the** Land of Luther," etc. 32mo, cloth, gilt edges. **Price 1s. 6d. Paste grain. Price 3s. 6d.**

The Bible Birthday Record. A Text-book for the Young. **By** the Author of "Hymns **from the** Land of Luther," etc. 32mo, cloth, gilt edges. **Price 1s. 6d.** Paste grain. Price **3s. 6d.**

The Imitation of **Christ** Birthday Book. With Scripture Texts and Selections from Thomas à Kempis. **Edited** by the Author of "Hymns from the Land of Luther." 32mo, cloth extra, gilt edges. Price 1s. 6d.

The Chaplet of Flowers. A **Daily** Text-book. Interleaved. **Cloth** extra, gilt edges. Price 1s. **6d.**

Daily Manna for Christian Pilgrims. A Daily Text - book. Interleaved. Cloth extra, gilt edges. **Price 1s.** 6d.

Daily Self-Examination. A Daily Text-book. Interleaved. Cloth **extra,** gilt edges. Price 1s. 6d.

Green Pastures. By the late **Rev.** JAMES SMITH. A Daily **Text**-book. Interleaved. Cloth **extra,** gilt edges. Price 1s. 6d.

Still Waters. By the late Rev. JAMES SMITH. A Daily Text-book. Interleaved. Cloth extra, gilt edges. Price 1s. 6d.

Words in Season for Young Disciples. A Daily Text-book. Interleaved. Cloth extra, gilt edges. Price 1s. 6d.

Daily Help in the Way of Holiness. By the Rev. JOHN DWYER. Interleaved. Cloth **extra,** gilt edges. Price 1s. 6d.

Help by the Way. A Daily Monitor. By A. M. **F.,** Author of "Bible Echoes," etc. With Introduction by the Rev. CHARLES BULLOCK, Rector of St. Nicholas, Worcester. Interleaved. Cloth **extra,** gilt **edges.** Price 1s. 6d.

The leading and distinctive feature of this volume is, that the art of questioning is brought to bear upon the daily text. The reader is thus made, by self-examination, to apply to his own conscience the scriptural truths enforced.

The Souvenir. **A Daily** Text-book. By H. **L. L.** Royal 18mo, gilt edges, cloth antique. Price 1s. 6d.

Daily Thoughts. A Text-book from the Psalms. Cloth antique, red edges. Price 1s.

Parent's Text-book for Young Children. Cloth antique, red edges. **Price 1s.**

The Souvenir. A Daily Text-book. Edited by H. L. L. Cloth antique, red edges. Price **1s.**

Bogatsky's Golden Treasury. Edited and Enlarged by the late Rev. JAMES SMITH. 24mo, cloth. **Price 1s. 6d.** 32mo. Price 1s.

Daily Bible Readings for the Lord's Household. Intended for the Family Circle or the Closet. By the Rev. JAMES SMITH, Author of "The Believer's Triumph," "Welcome to Jesus," etc. *Large Type Edition.* Post 8vo, cloth. Price 2s. 6d.

T. NELSON AND SONS, LONDON, EDINBURGH, AND NEW YORK.